I0565852

INVALID EVIDENCE

What Reviewers Say About Stevie Mikayne's Work

UnCatholic Conduct

"…very well written with good pacing, and a nice way to spend a rainy Saturday afternoon."—*The Romantic Reader Blog*

"*UnCatholic Conduct* moves smoothly and Mikayne layers her story with different reveals. We're not sure Pope Francis will be reading this novel, but you will definitely want to."—*Lambda Literary*

"…well plotted with a mystery that held my interest and had some surprising twists and turns."—*Library Thing*

Illicit Artifacts

"This book is damn good. It's a mystery that is tangled in so many ways, that at times I felt myself pull back and wonder how the author is going to pull this off. She did!"—*The Romantic Reader Blog*

"I enjoyed the unraveling of the mystery and it was well told and full of surprises. Jil's relationship with Jess, an in-the-closet Catholic School Principal, was tense and touching and I didn't know where it was going from chapter to chapter. I knew where I wanted it to go though. I enjoyed this book and want to go back and read the first in the series now."—*Inked Rainbow Reads*

Visit us at www.boldstrokesbooks.com

By the Author

UnCatholic Conduct

Illicit Artifacts

Invalid Evidence

INVALID EVIDENCE

by

Stevie Mikayne

2018

INVALID EVIDENCE

ISBN 13: 978-1-63555-307-9

This Trade Paperback Original Is Published By
Bold Strokes Books, Inc.
P.O. Box 249
Valley Falls, NY 12185

First Edition: December 2018

CREDITS
Editor: Cindy Cresap
Production Design: Susan Ramundo
Cover Design By Tammy Seidick

Dedication

To my travel-loving family. Tiny house, big adventures.

.

CHAPTER ONE

"Well, you can't say I never send you anywhere inter-esting," Padraig said.

Jil grabbed her latte off the bar and followed Padraig out the door to the coffee shop. The wind caught her scarf, and she shoved it back into the collar of her black trench coat.

For April, the weather was still cool and windy, but the sun was trying to shine, at least, and after six months of bleak gray snow, she was happy for that slight glimmer of light.

Padraig stopped on the street corner and pressed the walk button, then took off the lid to his black coffee and tossed it in the garbage can. "Don't know why the hell they put those damn lids on. Coffee never cools down."

Jil took a careful sip of her latte. She knew exactly why they put lids on. To keep people like her from sloshing their drinks all down their clothes. They made a turn, directly into a wind tunnel. And there it was, the April wind that felt like ice shards on her face. She wished he would just turn around and go back to the office.

Padraig turned to look at her while they waited for the light to turn. He looked pleased with himself.

"Out with it," Jil demanded.

"St. Emeline." Padraig beamed.

Jil frowned. "Where is that?"

"Just north of Curacao, below St. Martin. It's a pretty little island. You'll enjoy it, I think."

A wind gust kicked up, and she shivered despite the sun. Maybe heading south wouldn't be so bad.

"Someone from the Caribbean hired us? Why?"

Padraig smiled even wider. "Well, first of all, she doesn't trust the gendarme in St. Emeline. Apparently, there's some sort of conflict of interest there. You'll have to get the details yourself. And secondly, she's Canadian. From Rockford originally. She owns a sea aquarium on St. Emeline."

"I've never even heard of St. Emeline."

The light changed and Padraig began walking. "That's because you're living a sheltered life, Kidd. You need to travel more. Break out."

Jil snorted. "Oh, I forgot I was speaking to the ultimate globetrotter. When was the last time you even took a vacation?"

People crushed past them, and Jil almost lost her latte. It splashed around in her cup, bubbling up through the hole in the lid Padraig had eschewed, and streamed down her wrist. Her hands were so cold that she didn't really mind, but it would be sticky as hell once it cooled.

Padraig barreled on, unaware. When they got to the other side of the intersection, he kept walking, straight to the park. Usually Padraig could be counted on for a sit-down and a pint, not a power stroll through an icy street.

"It's technically not a vacation if you're solving a case."

"Maybe we could just sit down?"

Padraig finally looked at her, noticing the creamy froth dripping from her wrist.

"Sorry, Kidd." Hastily, he mopped at her hand with a crumpled napkin he took from his pocket. "Bench. Three o'clock."

He guided her to a fountain in Rockford's Coronation Park—a large circular basin with a concrete carving of an Inuit seal hunt erupting from the center.

Jil flashed back to her last case where she'd sat in this very spot and watched a jewel thief hand off her foster mother's emerald ring into the bottom of the empty fountain.

The fountain had been filled now in preparation for spring. The water flowed almost to the top.

Jil grabbed his elbow and stopped him from sitting in a splash of water on the stone bench. He moved over three spots and sat down, shaking his head.

"Why aren't you going yourself, then? Why are you sending me?"

Padraig looked at the ground. "Never mind. I have my reasons."

"Which are?"

"Has anyone ever told you you're bloody nosy sometimes?"

That stung.

"Sorry," Padraig muttered. "I didn't mean it like that. Me da's just died, if you must know."

"Your dad? I didn't even know he was still alive. You've never mentioned him. I just assumed…"

"Because I'm older than dirt, my parents must be long gone and buried? Believe me, I have no idea how the old bastard lived as long as he did, with as much as he drank. But maybe whiskey has the same effect as formaldehyde when taken in large enough doses. Anyway…"

"I'm sorry, Padraig."

"I am too. I know this news isn't going to come welcome to you, but it's got to be said, so…"

"What?"

He sighed and then took a big breath through his giant nostrils. Then sighed again.

"Ah, well, I may as well tell you now as wait till you come back."

"What?"

"I've decided to retire."

Jil almost spat out her drink.

"Excuse me? What? You're not serious."

"I am."

She looked at him doubtfully, but the downturn of his mouth told her he was serious.

"What? Why?"

"Don't you think I deserve some vacation time at my age? A membership to the seniors' center, maybe? Time for the casino?"

She shoved him. "Hardly."

"Fine. I might have an ulterior motive. I'll be at a funeral while you're sunbathing. Then I have to go sort through the old man's affairs. Probably never took care of a single piece of paperwork ever in his life. Plus, I'd like to enjoy my golden years, you know?"

He patted his midsection and sighed. "Doc says I've got to drop a few pounds to go easier on my ticker. She gave me this contraption." He opened his jacket to reveal something that looked like a tiny black pocket watch.

"A Fitbit?" Jil laughed. She tapped the screen. "Padraig, you've only got two thousand steps and it's already eleven o'clock."

"It's been a slow day."

Jil rolled her eyes. "That's why you dragged me out here? Shit's sake."

"I knew you'd want to help me live a long and healthy life." He glowered and she laughed harder.

"So that's why…what's going to happen to the firm?" Her stomach went cold. "My job?"

Padraig patted her hand. "Don't worry about that just now. Take a vacation first."

So that's why he was giving her this assignment. Guilt.

He fished in his black satchel and handed her a blue folder.

She set her coffee on the bench between then. It tipped and Padraig caught it before it fell off.

"Jaysus Murphy, girl."

"I'm sorry! God." Jil moved the coffee back onto a level surface and set the file in her lap. She flipped to page one. And the wind took it right out of her hands.

A gust rippled through the park, catching the pages from her folder and whipping them around.

She sprang up to catch them—one landed in the fountain, two in the treetops. She snatched up the papers closest to her and shoved them into her satchel.

Padraig ran in the opposite direction.

She didn't even wait to see if he'd retrieved them. Just shouted over her shoulder as she stalked off.

"You're getting a treadmill! And I'm going back to the office. While I still have a job."

Once she'd cleaned up and had a snack, she felt a little less like ripping up the case file, and a little more like reading it. How could Padraig retire? Just like that? What would she do without him? Why hadn't he mentioned that he was thinking about giving it up?

She rolled her eyes. She knew exactly why he hadn't said something. Because he hadn't wanted her to freak out, wondering what she was going to do with her life, which is what she was doing right now.

She forced herself back to work, scanning the pages. A young woman had been killed by an orca at the sea aquarium.

She flipped the pages and scanned the evidence.

Possibly.

Her interest finally piqued, she pulled out her phone.

"Call Jess."

"Calling Jess Blake."

Her partner answered on the second ring.

"Am I going to like this or not?"

Jil grinned. "Well…it depends on how you feel about the Caribbean."

Jess laughed. "I won't say I hate it. Where are we going?"

"St. Emeline. I know you've probably never heard—"

"Oh, I love St. Emeline."

Jil threw up her hands. "Okay, so apparently I'm the only person in the world who needs to go back and study high school geography."

"When do we leave?"

Padraig appeared at the door, waving something in her direction.

She squinted.

Plane tickets. The bribing bastard.

Saturday, he mouthed.

Jil rolled her eyes.

"You'd better pack your suitcase," she said to Jess. "Looks like we're on our way this weekend."

CHAPTER TWO

I've never heard of pre-tanning," Jil complained as Jess pointed to a small dirt road coming up on their right. She steered the car uphill, sending small rocks flying into the undercarriage.

"You'll be glad you did when you're not turning into a lobster on the beach your first day out," Jess replied. She opened the pamphlet on her lap. "There are twenty-seven features in this spa. Some hot, some cold. Something called a volcanic rock bed?"

Jil winked. "I hope it has a few dark corners."

Jess shoved her. "Stop it. We'll have plenty of that on our vacation!"

"Yeah. And we'd better enjoy it since I'll soon be unemployed."

Jess turned away.

"What?" Jil demanded.

But Jess shook her head and tried to smile. "Nothing. We'll handle it."

"Not sure how." Jil gripped Jess's elbows. "So can we just not think about it for now, please?"

That was a good idea. Jess knew that Jil had always counted on her job. Not for the money as much as for the outlet. The immersion of solving cases, following clues. It was the one thing she was good at. But without Padraig, what the hell was she going to do? She wasn't cut out to work for anyone else. She still needed a mentor to keep her out of trouble. Constant trouble.

"Is it just me or has life been way too busy lately?"

Jess sighed. "Well, you certainly have been. Me…not so much."

Jil patted her thigh. "I think we should use some of our vacation time to help you figure out your next step. Um, and mine, apparently. What do you think?"

With a long sigh, Jess nodded. "It's about time, yeah. In the meantime, I've been looking into our case."

"Our case, huh?" Jil grinned at her.

"Well, since I'm coming along, I might as well be useful."

"Good thing one of us is organized. I haven't even cracked the file since the day I got it. Too busy thinking about what snorkel gear to get!"

Jil parked and got out. Jess waited until she was headed up the path before she opened her door and slowly swung her legs out. Today would be a good experiment on heat and cold—which made things worse, which might help.

"All right, what did you find out?" Jil asked, taking her arm.

"Well, the sea aquarium has gone through several owners since it first opened in the early nineties. The current owner has had it for the past ten years. And in addition to being a world-famous attraction, it's also home to a famous dolphin therapy center."

"Oh. Neat. Who do the dolphins therapize?"

Jess tried to remember what the web site had said. "People with special needs, mostly. Kids with autism or other disabilities. They're closed every morning to accommodate their therapy programs. Open to the public in the afternoons. The owner, Rebecca-somebody is a physiotherapist."

"That's interesting. Are we tanning first or last?"

Jess flipped the itinerary the right way around as she followed Jil up the ramp to the main doors.

"Last."

"Well, then I want to find this volcanic heat bed."

They made their way to the change rooms and slipped out of their winter coats.

She turned to see Jil staring at her in the light from the window.

"You're like the definition of a whiter shade of pale, Jess."

Jess just gave her a look as she stripped off her jeans.

"Yeah, well, not all of us like to spend every waking moment in the sun when it's thirty below."

"You look like Casper. Seriously. I don't even think you can tan for five minutes."

Jess looked down at her thighs. Yikes. Almost luminescent. She never tanned well to begin with, but she had barely been outside in the past year, since her rheumatoid arthritis had really begun to limit her mobility.

"Maybe I'd better go with the shortest of the short sessions," she said.

Jil laughed.

"Why is it so dead in here?"

"Gee, I don't know. Maybe Wednesday morning at the spa is not on everyone's to-do list. Maybe they're, for example, at work."

She tried to keep the disappointment out of her voice, but she obviously didn't succeed, because Jil put her arms around her and kissed her forehead.

"You're not getting put out to pasture yet. So don't worry about it. You'll be back to work soon. Okay?"

Jess just sighed, not meeting her eye, as she took off her bra and panties and pulled on her bikini bottoms.

She looked up to see Jil's tight nipples pointing through her sporty tankini.

"Hm," she said.

Jil shot her a wry look. "What? It's been a while, you have to admit."

Jess felt a stab of guilt. "Not that long."

"Um yeah. Forever, actually."

Jess bit her lip and reached up a thumb to gently circle Jil's nipple through the tight black fabric.

Jil closed her eyes and Jess pushed her back gently against the locker as she planted a kiss on her clavicle.

"Well, if I'd known that all it took was a trip to the spa, I would have booked us in weeks ago," Jil muttered.

Jess traced her thumb down Jil's side and slowly pulled back the waistband to her bikini bottoms. She slipped her hand inside—

And the door banged open. A group of college girls barreled in, giggling their way to the showers. Jess extracted her hand. "Later," she whispered. "Let's go.

Jil groaned and followed her out the doors to the outdoor path, pulling on her white plush robe as she went. The whole spa was designed in the Nordic style, with wide wooden beams and flagstone paths, waterfalls cascading freezing streams of water into the cold features, and huge, hot spring rock baths.

Jess looked at the canvas hammocks, lined with fleece. "I want to try that," she announced.

"Good idea, but if we start there, I'm never getting out, so what about we start with something torturous and make our way back?"

Jess shivered in her white terry robe. "You're supposed to follow the arrows and alternate hot and cold. First the waterfall, then the hot tub. Then the ladle dip, whatever that is. And then the...I can't pronounce this."

Jil peered over her shoulder. "No idea. It sounds like an IKEA couch. Let's figure it out when we're sitting in the hot springs."

"Deal."

Jess kicked off her flip-flops and plunged into the icy pool. "Gah. That's terrible!" she gasped.

Jil followed close behind, beating her to the waterfall that cascaded down the rock face. "Ohmygod."

Jess stood shivering, her skin on fire. She wasn't sure if the cold water was making her joint pain better or just distracting her by short-circuiting her whole body. "I'm not ducking under that." Her lower jaw shuddered violently.

Jil disappeared under the waterfall and stuck her hand out. "Come on," she called. Her voice was muffled by the roar.

Jess groaned and plodded through the icy water. She grinned when she spotted a loophole. In a second, she had slipped behind the waterfall and poked Jil.

She jumped. "Where did you come from?"

"I went around!"

Jess showed her the side exit and they stumbled back out the stone steps, then hurried to the hot feature.

"I really don't think we need to follow the suggested route here," Jil said. Her lips were still blue.

Jess sank down into the stone seat, hot water lapping at her shoulders. She still hadn't stopped shivering.

"I agree. I think walking from hot tub to hot tub will cleanse our systems enough. Or whatever it's supposed to do."

Jess watched Jil dip her head back, extending her arms along the stone wall. She was still tanned, even after the brutal winter they'd had. And her fingernails badly needed a manicure.

"What are you worrying about?" she asked.

Jil looked up. "Nothing, why?"

Jess picked up one of Jil's hands. "Because you only bite your nails this badly when you're solving a case, and since the case hasn't started yet..."

Jil sighed. "And it might be the last one I get for a while."

Jess felt a clunk at the pit of her stomach. They couldn't both be out of work. They'd be broke as well as stir-crazy.

"It's Padraig. Why is he taking an extended leave now? He and his dad weren't close. I don't buy that he needs to take several weeks to clear out his decrepit house. He can hire someone for that if he wants to. He loves working. He needs work."

"Maybe he really is just trying to take care of his health," Jess said.

Jil shot her a look. "The man has had two pints with lunch the entire time I've known him. He's never eaten a vegetable. Never taken exercise. And now he's got a FitBit that he can barely operate. No. Something's up."

Jess laid a hand on her shoulder. "Well…I suppose there's only one thing to do."

Jil looked at her. "What?"

"Ask him!"

The teenagers from earlier were heading for the hot tub, and Jess rolled her eyes. They reminded her too much of her students.

Luckily, Jil seemed to read her mind and was already heading for the stairs.

As Jess took her time getting out, Jil had already read the map.

"Come on." Jil flashed her a smile and pointed toward a nearby building. Jess shoved her feet into her flip-flops, threw her robe around her shoulders, and followed Jil to the low building with faded red siding.

Inside, once the door had closed, the silence was total. A dark heat filled the space, not steamy or dry like the saunas, but almost sizzling. And it was dark. For a moment, they stood by the closed door, waiting until their eyes adjusted.

"Here, I see some lower ones," Jil whispered.

But Jess pulled Jil toward the ladder. "I want to go up."

Jess climbed up, hand over hand, to the top bunk, then slid in next to Jil on the smooth molten stone. The heat was penetrating, stopping just shy of scorching her bare back.

On the other side of the room, a snore sounded over the spa music that issued from the hidden speakers—waterfalls and harps.

Jess giggled. Someone had obviously fallen asleep on one of the hotbeds below. As her eyes adjusted to the semi-darkness, she peered around the bottom beds.

The place was nearly empty.

Except for the snoring guy in the corner.

Jess tapped her shoulder and Jil turned around. Jess leaned over, cupping the back of her head as she pulled her in for a kiss. It was a bit of a tight squeeze for two, but Jil fit herself snugly into Jess's arms and surrendered to the insistent pressure of Jess's tongue on hers, the way her hair, still damp from their dip in the hot tub, brushed against Jess's neck.

She fisted her hand at Jil's hair, bit her lip gently—not enough to draw blood, but enough that Jil growled into her collarbone.

"Keep that up and we're not going to make it home."

Jess kissed her way up Jil's neck to her ear, where she whispered, "Yeah, we're not going to make it home."

Jess brushed her thumb along Jil's cheekbone as she kissed her deeply, the way Jil liked to tongue fuck. They kissed the way they talked—with a quick and easy rhythm, pulling back and searching, drawing each other out.

Jil pulled away a little. "We have to stop. I'm seriously going to have to come."

Jess squeezed her breast. "So come."

"Here? Honestly? What if—"

"I don't care."

The song on the spa music changed—this one including bells or chimes, or something. It didn't matter what, because it was slightly louder than the previous track and muffled the sound of Jil's moan when Jess reached behind her and undid her bikini top.

Jil's breast arched right into Jess's mouth, and Jess closed her lips gently over the nipple.

She wasn't playing fair and she knew it, but something about the way Jil's body undulated like a piece of music when she was aroused made Jess want to play her. She was an instrument of legs and arms, and one hot, sweet center. Not unlike her cello.

She ran her fingers down Jil's skin, raking nails gently down her back, across her stomach.

"God," Jil whispered when Jess made contact with her bikini bottom. "I can't be quiet, Jess."

Jess sealed her mouth over Jil's and kissed her hard, dragging her nails down over the wet bathing suit, across Jil's hard clit that pulsed under the swatch of Lycra.

Jil moaned into Jess's mouth. A long, breathy sigh with a harder edge of need.

Jess knew that noise. Knew when Jil was hitting the brink of orgasm.

"Fuck."

At the sound of the voice from below, they both froze. The snoring man jumped up from his hot bed and stormed out, the door banging behind him.

Jess giggled. "What the hell was that about?"

Jil moved her hips so Jess's fingers were snugly against her clit.

"I guess he didn't mean to fall asleep." Her voice was edgy, tense.

Jess knew why. Her own body was ablaze, every single nerve on end and heated by the lava bed and Jil's breasts pressed against her body.

She pulled Jil's bikini bottom down and helped her work it free, then wiggled back up beside her and worked her fingers in slow circles against Jil's clit. Jil moaned out loud.

If anyone happened to come in right now, they'd be in for a show, but Jess didn't care, and she doubted Jil did either at this moment.

She nudged Jil's legs open with her knee, and Jil obliged, ready for Jess's fingers that curled into her, homing in on her G-spot as she maintained a steady rhythm on her clit with her thumb.

Jil arched back and squeezed around Jess's fingers, urging her to go deeper.

Jess pulled out slowly and pushed back in firmly until Jil came, a strangled moaning against Jess's shoulder.

CHAPTER THREE

Saturday morning, Jil woke up to a cold, steady drizzle against the loft window. She rolled over and smacked her alarm clock then rolled back and noticed the empty bed.

The smell of coffee alerted her to where Jess might have gone.

She turned on her phone and waited for the messages to load. The first one, predictably, was from Padraig, giving her a meter-long list of last-minute instructions.

"Have you seen Blackfish*? Maybe you should start with that. If you're not squeamish."*

She rolled her eyes. She'd been watching it last night, scrutinizing all the details of whales that killed their trainers. In some of the conditions, she couldn't say she blamed the creatures. And maybe, for once, the surface story that someone gave her would turn out to be the actual truth. She'd arrive on St. Emeline, find out that a whale had indeed gone justifiably murderous, and say toodle–oo to the case, leaving her and Jess free to enjoy the beach for the rest of the trip.

But her gut feeling was that something didn't add up. Jess arrived, bearing coffee, and she reached out with both hands.

"Life."

"Sorry to be the bearer of bad news, but there's a note in the mail."

Jil took the envelope from her and ripped it open.

...hereby give notice that the unit will be up for sale in two months' time.

Her stomach lurched.

"Oh my God."

"What?"

"It's a notice from the owners. They're selling the loft."

Jess sat down on the edge of the bed. "When?"

"Two months' notice."

Jess squeezed her hand, the breath whooshing out of her. "Wow."

Jil threw back the covers and got out of bed.

"I guess I'll be adding house-hunting to my post-vacay to-do list. Jesus."

She stalked across the room and slammed the bathroom door.

❖

"Got everything?" Jil swung her suitcase over the couch and stacked it in the front hall.

Zeus whined and stomped at the door.

"Just this left." Jess began to drag her wheeled suitcase down the stairs, but Jil sprinted up and grabbed it from her. "I've got it."

Jess let it go and sighed, then pulled her purse over one shoulder and snagged her coat from the top banister.

"I can hear your thoughts. Don't even go there," Jil said. She slapped Jess's suitcase down beside hers and reached for the car keys.

Jess bent slowly to pick up Zeus's leash from the basket by the door. She straightened up, wincing, and Jil stopped where she was, fixing her with a look.

"You have a doctor's appointment as soon as we get back, right?"

"Yeah." Jess took a breath in, smiling wanly. "Stop worrying."

"I'm going to worry."

"Seems like a lot of effort, considering that there's nothing that can be done. You're sure you want to love a woman with a chronic debilitating disease?"

"Fuck that shit," Jil said. "You're too young to be crippled." She kissed Jess lightly on the forehead.

"Don't I know it."

"One day at a time. Today, we take a vacation."

"I can't even remember the last time I had a vacation," Jess said. "The plane ride's going to be interesting."

"I got you an aisle seat, don't worry. Booked it this morning."

Jess grabbed her arm and kissed her—impulsively, deeply. "I love you," she said when she pulled away.

Jil stopped and looked back at her, then hugged her tight. "Likewise," she whispered into her hair. "I adore you. I just want to get there so I can lay you down on some hot sand and..."

Jess laughed and pressed her hand up Jil's shirt into the bare small of her back. "Tell me on the plane," she said.

Jil kissed her again and headed for the door.

"What time's the dog sitter coming for Zeus?"

"He said he'd be here at four."

Jess checked her watch. "It's four thirty now."

Jil rolled her eyes. "Well, I guess he's on his way. Either that or Zeus will be coming with us to St. Emeline."

Jess laughed. "I think he's over the weight restriction."

"Yeah, by about fifty percent."

"He is getting rather large," Jess said. "Even for a Dane."

"His chest." Jil scratched the patch of white below Zeus's collar and he leaned into her. "It's like the broad side of a barn."

Jess laughed. "Next time get a Chihuahua. At least those are allowed in a carry-on."

Zeus looked at her.

"Oh, I'm sorry. You know we wouldn't trade you for fifteen rat dogs. And you're going to have a great time." Jess scratched behind his ears and clipped the leash on him. "Let's go."

In another hour, Zeus had left, they had thrown their bags in the car, and they were in gridlock traffic, heading for the airport.

"Fucking rush hour's getting worse by the day," Jil said. She inched up half a centimeter as the car ahead of her crawled forward.

Two right-hand lanes closed. Expect delays.

"I think we're going to miss the flight," Jess said mildly.

"And that's why we're leaving tonight and not tomorrow morning. There are a thousand flights from here to Toronto, but only one out to St. Emeline tomorrow."

"Is it that remote?"

"I think it's just the off-season thing," Jil said. "There are only two airlines who fly in and out from Canada. One on a Friday, one on a Sunday."

"I'm glad not to have two flights in the same day anyway."

Jil looked over at her. She was pale still, her hands balled into fists, whether or not she realized it. The stress line between her eyes was getting deeper, and she clenched her teeth in her sleep. If anyone needed a vacation from this past year, it was Jess.

Maybe the distance would help her to make some of the decisions that had been weighing on her mind so heavily these past few months. Whether to give up her principalship and start a new career. To finally pursue a divorce. To sell the house she'd shared with Mitch before his accident. To start living the life she deserved, shucking the guilt that sat on her like a lead blanket in the heat of summer.

Every day.

The crawling traffic slowed even further until everyone seemed to be at a dead stop.

The sign above changed to read *Accident ahead. Expect delays.*

Jess shifted in her seat, then pulled the lever to recline a little. "Sorry to abandon you," she said. "I'm getting a little stiff sitting here."

Realizing they hadn't actually moved in the past five minutes, Jil put the car into park and shut off the engine.

"Maybe we should call the airline."

Jess pulled out her cell phone and dialed, then punched through the automated system and waited.

Jil tapped the steering wheel and looked over at Jess. Her shirt had ridden up just enough to show a thin line of midriff. She traced a finger across Jess's stomach, ending on her opposite hip.

Jess shot her a look and pushed a tongue into her cheek, then turned her attention back to her conversation, purposely avoiding Jil's eyes.

"Yes, hello. We're on the six eighteen flight from Rockford to Toronto and we're stuck in traffic. We're not going to make it, unfortunately. We'd like a later flight, please. Yes, I'll hold."

Jil kept one eye on the traffic—not moving—and stole a glance at Jess as she flicked open the button on her low-rise jeans.

"Jillienne Kidd and Jessica Blake," Jess said, eyeing Jil warily.

Jil lowered Jess's zipper.

Jess stared at her and shook her head, mouthing *don't you dare*.

"You needed a stretch you said."

Jil nudged her leg and Jess relented. Slowly, she reclined the chair even farther, biting her lower lip.

Jil popped open Jess's seat belt and glanced once again at the gridlock traffic. They'd be lucky if they moved half a kilometer in the next hour.

"Yes, we'll take the seven thirty."

Deciding to put their tinted windows to the test, Jil leaned over and slid one hand inside Jess's jeans. With a short lift of her hips, Jess parted her legs to let her in. Jil pushed past her panties, noting the gorgeous navy blue lace.

"Well, we'd prefer to sit together if possible. If not, we'll take two singles."

Jess arched back into the headrest, her hips pressing into the seat as Jil began flicking lightly.

"Thank you," she said, struggling to keep her voice steady. "Yes, I'll hold."

"You might want to put that on mute," Jil suggested.

Jess shot her a look, but muted her phone and put it on speaker so the elevator music played out into the car as Jil continued to touch her, spreading her hot juices over her hardening clit.

"I don't think we're having enough sex," Jil mused.

"No?" Jess managed breathlessly. "Because you can get me off in less than thirty seconds?"

"Well, that might be all we have."

"I don't think it'll be a problem."

Jess moaned as Jil hit the side of her clit, drawing out her pleasure zone into an ever-widening circle. "I'm just going to close my eyes and think of you at the spa."

Jil grinned and ran her finger up one side and down the other while Jess cursed under her breath.

It wouldn't even take thirty seconds, Jil realized, as Jess's clit began to throb under her finger. She circled around and Jess closed her eyes, moaning.

"Ms. Blake?"

Jess's eyes flew open and Jil stopped touching her long enough for her to answer the phone.

"Yes?" her voice was barely a whisper.

"You're all set. See you at seven thirty."

"Thank you." Jess pressed the end button and looked up.

"More?" Jil said sweetly.

Jess covered Jil's hand with her own, nudging her back into place. "Please finish before I die."

Jil smiled and ran her finger back up and down, circling out and in, firmly, gently, drawing Jess out.

She moved her hips up and back, the gentlest and most effective stretching exercise possible, and Jil touched her, a hot, sweet caress, until Jess came with a quiet, "Fuuuuck."

Chapter Four

As the plane taxied to the runway, a wave of phones came out, and passengers began clicking and messaging, holding their phones up for reception.

Jess rolled her eyes. "We're on vacation, right?"

"Absolutely," Jil said. "I may not even have packed my phone."

"Liar. It's in your carry-on."

Jil laughed. "So's yours."

Jess sighed and shot her a look. "I used to need mine. I wonder what it'll be like to be so unneeded."

Floating. Free-falling through life. No anchor, no ties.

Jil squeezed her arm. "That'll last five minutes at the most."

"I hope so."

The airlock opened and a blast of air swept in, so heavy with moisture it almost swam over them.

Jess pushed out of her seat and took a moment to stretch her legs and arms before reaching for their overhead luggage. The air smelled salty and fresh. She couldn't wait to get out. A vacation. Beach and oceanfront. Maybe a massage in the sand.

Jil pulled her T-shirt away from her chest and slipped her feet into the flip-flops she'd brought on the plane.

"Vacation time. Let's get going."

Jess maneuvered her way down the aisle, holding on to the back of the seats. She felt Jil squeeze in behind her and knew instinctively that she was bracing Jess against the crush of people rushing for the exit.

She always did that—physically moved in to cover the gaps. Fill the holes. Stretch to the places where Jess worried about going.

She breathed out, focusing on navigating the narrow space without feeling like she was being propelled out of the plane.

They joined the throng of people moving through the small airport and down to customs. The line was already thousands deep. Jess sighed and tried to focus on the incremental steps forward and not the screaming protest of her hip joints.

"Hey, did you see that?"

She pointed to a newsstand and Jil squinted, her gaze zeroing in on the image of an orca with its jaws open wide.

"That was so sad," said a voice behind them.

They turned around to see an older woman looking in the same direction. Her white dreadlocks were tied back in a loose ponytail and her yellow dress swayed with her as she talked.

"Knew that girl's mother. We was friends in school."

Jil turned. "What happened?"

The woman shook her head. "Tasha. Beautiful girl. Mad animal lover, ever since she was in diapers. Used to be down at the beach, making animals out of sand instead of castles. Once, she made a whale. It took her all day. All day. And then the tide came in and it started washing away the tail. Oh, was she mad."

Her eyes crinkled as she smiled.

"And she went to work at the sea aquarium?" Jil asked.

"Yes. Graduated her college course and went for her internship. Oh, she was so excited. We had a party for her on the street. A vegetarian fry-up. It was her favorite. Wouldn't even eat fish, that girl." She laughed.

The line moved forward again. They were halfway to the end, Jess noticed. She took a few deep breaths and focused on the woman's story.

"She started with the animal tanks. Cleaning lobsters and crabs and things. But what she really wanted to do was mammals. The dolphins and the whales. Loved that whale, Tsunami. She worked so many hours, just sitting there on the platform. Just waiting for her to come. She never believed she purposely hurt that other trainer in Curacao."

Jess and Jil exchanged a look.

"When she took a fish from her, Tasha was so happy. So happy. Came home dancing."

She stopped talking. She rummaged in her purse for a mint and focused on unwrapping it slowly. Her nose had gotten red.

"Then what happened?" Jil asked gently.

The woman sighed. The line moved forward.

"It's not for me to say," she said, nearly a whisper. "Nothing but rumors."

Jil waited.

The line moved forward again.

The old woman sighed. "She was with a boy. Her mother didn't like him. That's all."

"Why didn't she like him?"

"He was older. He took too many risks, not like Tasha." She took a deep breath, pressing the Kleenex to her nose. "We all miss her, that's all."

"I can't imagine," Jil said.

Jess watched the way she stood close, but not crowding the old woman. The way she put one hand on the woman's shoulder.

"And then last week, her mother got the call. She'd been killed at the sea aquarium. One of the saddest days I can remember for a long time."

The line had opened. The woman gestured toward the booth.

"Looks like it's your turn."

"Next!"

"Where can we find you, if we feel like a tour of the island?"

The woman pulled out a card. "Here. Look me up."

Margot's Fish Restaurant.

They moved to the counter, giving the woman a wave over their shoulders. She lifted her chin in parting and they moved through Customs and into the circus of luggage claim.

Everyone was moving around the carousel, grabbing suitcases and duffel bags. A whistle pierced the air and a hound pulled on its lead, darting in and out of luggage. It leaped over carts, smelling, trotting, and finally sat down next to a large blue bag.

Two women in crisp, short-sleeved uniforms and caps closed in and took the bag.

A young man with wide eyes watched them.

"Is this yours?"

He nodded.

"Come with us, please."

Meanwhile, Jil had loaded their luggage onto a cart. Now she grabbed Jess's arm and pulled her out into the waiting taxi stand.

"What was that?"

Jil shrugged. "Drugs, I guess? Maybe chocolate bars?"

She remembered being snagged by a police dog when she got off a plane in Auckland, a half-eaten Oh Henry still in her purse. "You never know what a country is particular about."

The sun was almost white in the sky, and Jess began to sweat.

"You doing okay?" Jil asked.

"I'll be glad to get there."

They scanned the crowd, looking for their names.

"There."

A short man with black hair and a wide smile waved as they approached.

"You must be Jil."

"I am."

"I'm Ramone."

Jess liked him. His accent was so mixed that she couldn't identify where he was from, but his smile went all the way into the crinkles of his forehead, and she grinned.

"I work for the sea aquarium. I'll be taking you ladies to your hotel."

He led them to a Jeep that looked like it had been on the road before they were born.

Jil helped Jess into the front seat, then swung herself through the back window and onto the back bench.

"You must be able to eat a horse."

Jil and Jess exchanged a look. "Um, yeah, I'm hungry," Jil admitted.

Jess realized her own stomach was rumbling too.

Ramone grinned. "Good. Then let me introduce you to my mother."

He pushed the pedal to the floor, and soon they were winding down a pothole-covered road, in and out of vegetation that alternated between cacti and the most luscious leaves Jess had ever seen. He banked a hard right and skidded to a stop outside a blue-sided hut. They were hit with the smell of cinnamon and sugar.

Jess's mouth watered. "What is that?"

"Churros."

An old woman with a braid of white hair and a missing front tooth waved at them.

"Hola."

"My mother," Ramone said. "Have a seat."

He approached the window and said something in Spanish. A child popped out from a lower cupboard. He held an old style Polaroid camera and closed one eye as he snapped their picture.

"What did I tell you about that?" Ramone said. "Ask before you take pictures of strangers! They might not like it. And don't waste that film. It's expensive!"

"Sorry, Papa."

"Never mind sorry. Just remember what I tell you."

He pulled the young boy out of the trailer and plunked him down on one of the two picnic tables in the yard.

"Come. Sit. Meet my son, Emilio."

"Emi," said the boy. He grinned, and his smile was exactly like his father's.

"Hi," Jess said.

"Hi. Sorry I took your picture without asking."

"Can I see it?"

He waved it expertly to help the development process, an action that reminded Jess of her childhood when Polaroids were all the rage.

Apart from her half-closed eyelids, and Jil's hair covering her face, it wasn't a bad photo.

Jil looked at it and laughed. "Don't quit your day job, kid."

"Don't quit your day job…" Ramone mused over this, like he'd just been given a new piece of jewelry.

"It means that…"

Emi looked at her, eyebrows raised.

"Um…"

"It means," Jess cut in. "Keep practicing, kid. And one day you'll be a pro."

He grinned.

A few minutes later, they were presented with two steaming piles of cinnamon sugar churros and several scoops of vanilla ice cream.

Jil met her eyes. "Wow."

Ramone smiled. "Welcome to St. Emeline."

"Papa, you're going to work now?"

"Sí."

"I'm coming with you."

"No. I told you, you're staying with Abuela."

"But it's boring. I miss the dolphins. I miss swimming with Relay. And Tsunami needs her fish. It's my day job. I'm coming with you. Please, Papa."

"No. I'm not telling you again, Emilio. *Peligroso*. Hear me? You stay here."

The boy crossed his arms and sulked.

Jil leaned in. "What's *peligroso*?" she whispered.

Jess waited until Ramone had bent down to talk to the boy again, then whispered, "Dangerous."

By the time they arrived at their beachfront hotel, dusk had fallen and the beaches had emptied.

Jil raised her cocktail. A piece of pineapple pressed against a maraschino cherry balanced on the rim. "Cheers to the best working vacation ever."

Jess raised her glass and clinked it with Jil's. They each took a sip.

Jil's mouth puckered. "Gah. That's sweet."

"Holy crap, you're not kidding." Jess stuck out her tongue, gagging.

"Right, I'll open the wine then."

Jil headed to the kitchen, skidding in her flip-flops on the tile floor.

"Careful."

"This place is gleaming. I mean, look at this thing. What is it, a microwave or an oven?"

Jess watched her peering at the chrome rectangle set into the wall and suppressed a smile. Jil was not exactly known for her culinary skills. But this high-tech kitchen wasn't what she had expected from island life either.

"What time is it, anyway? The clock here says four a.m."

Jess laughed. "I'd venture to say that's incorrect. Hang on."

She reached for her phone and waited while it switched on.

"God, Jil, I have five messages."

Jil picked another piece of pizza out of the box on the counter and shot her a quizzical look.

"Who from?"

Jess opened the phone history. Rockford Memorial Hospital. Five missed calls.

She dialed in quickly to her voice mail. Scanned through the messages, each one increasing in urgency. She didn't even listen to the last one. Instead, she hung up, then dialed the hospital.

"Yes, this is Jessica Blake. Dr. Rabinovitch, please."

As she waited, tears pooled in her eyes. Was Mitch dying? Dead already?

She felt Jil come up behind her, and she leaned into her arms, letting Jil's strength hold her together for a moment.

"Jessica? It's Howie Rabinovitch."

"Howie. I'm in St. Emeline. I'm sorry it's taken me so long." She began to cry.

"Jessica. Hey, sweetie, not yet. We're not gonna cry yet, okay? Here's the problem."

Jess took the Kleenex that Jil handed her and held it to her nose. "Okay. Okay. Tell me."

"He's got an infection, okay? From two places. One is his PICC line and the other's his G-tube site. Not sure what's causing the problem here, but his fever spiked pretty high this afternoon which is why we were trying to get hold of you."

"Did it come down?"

"It did. The antibiotics seem to be working for now, but I'm not sure that's going to be a permanent solution."

"What else could happen?"

Dr. Rabinovitch sighed. She could picture his frown. His hands stroking his beard as he searched for words.

"I'm afraid what we might be looking at is sepsis, Jess. He's been immobile for a long time. The bedsores on his back and glutes are a constant battle. Now he's rejecting the G-tube and PICC line. I think it's only a matter of time."

Jess let it sink in. Imagined him lying there, his body turning on itself. "You mean he's dying."

"Not today," Dr. Rabinovitch said. "But yes, I think we need to talk about this. Soon. Discuss his final directives. When are you back?"

"We just landed," Jess whispered. She felt weak, sick. Jil held her closer. "I'm not sure when I can get back."

"Even if it's a few days, we've got some time," Dr. Rabinovitch said. "That's sort of what I'm getting at, Jess. This could go on for a long time if we let it. So we need to talk about whether or not we let it."

Jess hung up, then sank onto the couch. Ever since her husband's accident five years ago, she had been imagining this moment, preparing for it. The day when his coma would end and he would wake up, or his body would give up, and he'd die.

She breathed out a long breath. The pizza and sweet booze were not sitting well.

Jil squeezed her tight.

"How soon do you need to leave? I can get us a connecting flight tomorrow."

Jess nodded. "Yeah. Okay. Thank you." She pulled a pillow into her chest. From the kitchen came the sound of the kettle hitting the stovetop. The knob turning.

"He's dying, Jil."

"I'm so sorry, Jess. I know it's awful."

Jil grabbed her iPad and began typing and scrolling.

"Only one seat left in coach. Let me check business class."

Jess listened to the water heating, a slow rumble.

How soon would it be? How quickly could she get there?

"None left in business."

She looked up. "Coach is fine."

Jil looked at her. "There's just one seat left."

"Better take it then."

"Don't you want me to come with you?"

"No. You've got a job to do. You stay here."

Jil turned back to her iPad and punched in her credit card number. "We can call the airline in the morning and make the switch," she muttered. "But it's reserved for now."

"Thank you."

Chapter Five

Jil woke up at five. The first rays of pink were starting to gleam in the sky. Jess had spent most of the night up pacing or tossing and turning in the bed. Neither of them had slept very well.

She pulled her hair into a top knot as she left the cool air-conditioned bedroom for the humidity of the living space. Jess was on the balcony with a cup of coffee, watching the ocean.

Yesterday, they'd been so excited and full of vacation glee. Today, everything seemed bleak and lonely.

She poured herself a cup of coffee and headed out to the balcony.

"Hey."

Jess glanced up, then back at the ocean.

"Ramone texted to say he'd be here in a few minutes."

"Did you fill him in?"

Jil shook her head. "No. I wanted to make sure you didn't want me to come with you."

"What would be the point?" Jess snapped. "It's going to be bad enough for me to pace the hallways and wait."

Jil took a deep breath. Jess didn't mean to be hurtful. "That's why I thought maybe you could use some support," she said quietly.

With a small chuckle, Jess turned away. "Jil, I love you, but sitting still and playing the supporting role isn't exactly your strong suit. You'd better just stay and get the job done. Keep moving. That's what you're good at."

Jil just stood there for a moment. Mitch was a topic she couldn't touch, apparently. A past self, a past life, that had no place for Jil in it.

"What are you going to do, exactly?" she asked. "Sit and hold his hand?"

It came out far more sarcastic than she'd meant. Why had she said that?

Jess looked at her, shocked. "For a start," she said.

"Jess, you're going home to say good-bye to someone you loved. Or love." She realized she didn't even know how Jess felt about him. "Don't you think that's a place where you'd want your partner?"

Jess turned to face Jil. "You think I should bring my lesbian partner to the hospital where my comatose husband is dying? With my mother-in-law's pious prayer group breathing down our necks, reminding me of what a sinner I am? How I've desecrated the marriage vows I've made in the worst way? How I've betrayed my husband?"

Jil stepped back. "Is that what you think? Is that how you feel about us?"

Jess burst into tears. "No. Yes. I don't know. Some days. Only when I remember how badly things ended." She sat down on the beach chair, her head in her hands.

Jil sat down slowly beside her. "You know it takes two people to make a marriage dysfunctional, right?"

"Well, not really. I mean, I'm the one who's gay."

Jil looked at her. "Right. But he's the one who married a lesbian."

"That's not his fault."

"And it's not yours either."

Jess laid her head on Jil's shoulder. "I still feel guilty."

They looked out over the ocean, at the waves that were breaking on the white sand.

"I wish you were staying."

Jess sighed. "I do too. But I have to do this for him. I have to see that he's taken care of. You'll understand when you're married."

Jil stood up. "I kind of thought I was married," she said softly. She left Jess to finish her coffee and went back inside. Sitting at the table, she spread out her files, then grabbed her notebook and began to scribble everything she could remember from the woman's story she had heard yesterday at the airport. Reading it back, she wondered what she was even doing here.

She should just go home with Jess.

Clearly, that whale was a known problem.

She scrolled through the newspaper columns and articles, tracing Tsunami back to when she was a pup. There was even a record of her on the internet, and she stared at it before getting an idea.

She grabbed a roll of paper and commandeered one of the kitchen walls to begin making herself a giant white board. She drew on a timeline and plotted Tsunami's life from the time she was a pup up to the present moment, where she swam around in a holding tank at the St. Emeline Sea Aquarium.

Next, she added the incidents Tsunami had been involved in, at which tanks, and with which people...

A knock on the door interrupted her. She threw on a wrap and peeked out the peephole to find Ramone standing on her threshold.

"Good morning!" He beamed when she opened the door. "Ready for your day? We're going to have a whale of a time."

Beside him, Emilio giggled.

Jil rolled her eyes.

He grinned back.

Nerds—both of them.

"I've brought you ladies some fresh pastry. I'll be taking you to the sea aquarium. Consider me your chauffeur."

"I'm helping," Emilio said.

"But only for the drive," Ramone said sternly. "Right? Then you go with Abuela."

Emilio frowned. "Whatever," he muttered.

Jess appeared from the balcony. "Actually, I'll be heading to the airport."

Ramone's face fell. "So soon? You just got here."

"Bad news from home," Jil said tightly. "She's on the first plane out."

"Well, allow me to take you," Ramone said. He set the pastries on the hall table.

"That's okay—" Jil started to say, just as Jess said, "Thank you. That would be lovely."

She stared at Jess.

"I'll take you to the airport, Jess."

"You're busy, Jil. You came here to do a job, and from the sounds of it, you've got your work cut out for you. You'd better get started."

She headed into the bedroom and Ramone gave Jil a look.

"Hey! Does that mean we're going to the airport? Can we go in? Can we get some McDonald's? Please?"

Ramone rolled his eyes. "You just had two croissants."

"Yeah, but I didn't know I could get a hash brown."

"You've got a hollow leg, I see," Jil said.

Emi looked at her askance. "What?"

Ramone guffawed. "Hollow leg? I love it. You stick with me, I'll learn a lot."

"Well, you can add it to your nerd collection. It means you have a lot of storage space for food," she told Emi.

He nodded, thinking.

Another moment later, Jess appeared, rolling her suitcase behind her. She crossed the short distance between them and gave Jil a quick peck on the cheek.

"See you when you get home."

Ramone looked back at her, concern on his face, as he dragged Jess's suitcase out the door. "I'll send someone else to get you, Jil. Rebecca's expecting you in a few minutes."

Jess looked at her, as if to say *see, I told you so*.

"Don't worry about it," Jil said. "I can get there on my own."

"Are you sure? It's no problem."

"I'm sure. I could do with the exercise."

"Just head straight down to the top of this road and look for the giant whale up on a pole."

"Got it."

With an attempt at a smile, Ramone took Jess out to the car, Emi chattering beside him about the different types of breakfast sandwiches, and if he was too young to try coffee.

The door closed and Jil sank into a chair. She heard the Jeep roar out of the driveway and felt the thud of loneliness in the pit of her stomach.

She was by herself on a tropical vacation.

Great.

Her gaze landed on the bag Ramone had dropped on the front hall table and she got up to take out a *pain au chocolat*.

Why not?

She set a croissant on a plate and tinkered with the cappuccino machine until it began sputtering and foaming. She wondered how long it would take Jess to get home.

CHAPTER SIX

The WestJet plane sat on the tarmac, and Jess stared at it anxiously. She checked her watch. Still 10:35. Time hadn't even inched forward a minute. Passengers began trickling out the chute and past the glass walls, dragging carry-ons and carrying their shoes while flip-flopping their way across the airport carpet.

Her flight didn't leave for another hour. What could possibly take an hour? Luggage, passed hand to hand, made its way into the articulated luggage vehicles. What were those called? Mitch would know.

Jil would know too.

Suddenly, she wished Jil was sitting beside her, holding her hand.

That was impossible for so many reasons, and the sadness of it brought new tears to her eyes.

Mitch was dying. Dying.

But he'd been gone for years. Why was it a sudden shock?

Grief for the life they'd never have? The love they'd never share or had never shared? The morning she'd last seen him, which had played over and over in her mind for the last few years while he'd lain there, wasting away, the breathing machine ventilating him, in, out, in, out.

Now that memory would be replaced by his funeral.

There were no happy memories left.

Her phone bleeped and she looked down.

Text me when you board. And when you land. And when you're home. <3 J

She breathed out. She hated the way she and Jil had left things, but she couldn't let her come home. It wasn't fair to anybody. She texted back. *Still waiting. Plane is here.*

You're watching them load the baggage carts?

She smiled. *How'd you guess?*

They'll vacuum next and toss out the trash, then the plane's all yours. Safe flight. Try not to worry. I'm heading into the aquarium. TTYL.

Easier said than done, obviously.

She took her carry-on and headed for the bathroom. One last stop in a non-moving stall before negotiating the plane aisle. She hadn't had anything to drink this morning for just that reason, but still, it was five hours to Toronto and then another flight back to Rockford.

She slowly latched the door and sat on the toilet. What a fucking nightmare. Two overseas flights in forty-eight hours. Her body felt like it was being burned at the edges and crushed simultaneously.

The medication barely took the edge off.

Exacerbation was stress-related, of course, but it was hard to remember that when you were looking for an accessible stall with a tall toilet because you couldn't squat over a regular height one. At thirty-five years old.

She put her head in her hands and closed her eyes for a second.

A sound like a bike stopping outside the stall made her glance up.

She hurried to put herself together and rushed out of the stall, her bag behind her. A young woman in a racing wheelchair glared as Jess walked past.

But Jess refused to shoot her an apologetic look, as she normally would. She just rolled her eyes and headed for the sink.

"Asshole," the woman in the chair muttered.

"Excuse me?" Jess whirled around.

Normally, she'd ignore it. She'd say nothing; she'd accept that she didn't look at all disabled and thank God that she could still walk around on her own two feet.

"There're seventeen other stalls," said the young woman. Her eyebrow ring glinted as she glared.

"Yeah? Well, I need that one too, okay? You're not the only one with a disability."

The woman's eyebrows raised, carrying the glinting eyebrow ring toward her bangs, cut in a stylish rough crop. She couldn't be more than nineteen, twenty years old. One of Jess's students, in another time and place.

"Sorry. You're right, I shouldn't...it's just that so many people...I thought—"

Jess let out a breath. "Yeah, I know. I know what it looks like. But I'm not using it for kicks and giggles, believe me."

She washed her hands and yanked open the door. As she exited, pulling her bag over the lip of the carpet, one of the carry-on wheels twisted. She stumbled, the bag suddenly at an awkward angle, no longer rolling.

"Fantastic," she muttered.

"This is the advanced boarding call for flight five-five-eight to Toronto. All passengers who need extra assistance should now make their way to the desk."

She made her way to the line, dragging the bag, which was far too heavy to be carried. She reached down for her passport.

Which was not in her purse.

She opened her carry-on and rooted around. Not there either.

Because she'd left it on the counter of the bathroom along with her boarding pass.

"Final call for advanced boarding for flight five-five-eight."

She spun around and almost collided with the footrest of a wheelchair, half-falling in the lap of the woman from the bathroom. She braced her hand on the woman's shoulder so she didn't land on top of her, and in an awkward, fumbling tangle of hands and arms, the woman helped her back to standing.

"Sorry," Jess muttered. "I'm not going to stop making an ass out of myself with you today."

"No worries. Apparently, I was also an ass. Here." She held out Jess's passport. "You left this."

Jess shook her head. "An ass and an idiot." She smiled ruefully.

"And that was just in the bathroom."

In spite of the knot in her stomach, Jess actually laughed. "I'm Jessica."

"I know. I read your passport. I'm Georgette."

"Really?"

She looked at Jess quizzically. "Yeah. Why?"

"Unusual name."

"It was my grandmother's."

"I'm a principal. And I've never taught a Georgette. That really doesn't happen very often."

"Well, congratulations on having met one. I'm sure it was a fabulous experience for you." She grinned and Jess shook her head. Together they joined the end of the line of passengers traveling with small children.

"I've got to wait here," Georgette said when they reached the door of the plane. "This is the part where they rob me of my wheelchair and give me that ridiculous aisle-wheelbarrow."

Jess laughed. She'd seen one before.

"Sorry."

Georgette shrugged. "Life."

Jess waved and went on without her.

As she settled into her middle seat, her carry-on shoved precariously into the overhead bin, Jess felt tendrils of anxiety clenching around her until she felt like she wanted to scream. Another tin box. Another excruciating flight. Tears welled up in her eyes. Why was this happening to her?

Had she just been too busy working to notice it before, or had it been this bad for a long time?

Three rows behind her, a mother and her two kids squeezed into their seats, and an iPad began jangling loudly. The next minute, the aisle-wheelbarrow arrived next to her and Georgette waved.

"Ha."

Jess smiled. "Really? You're with me?"

"Guess they stick the crips together, eh?" She laughed. "Good luck to whoever wants that window seat."

The flight attendant helped Georgette into her seat.

"Listen," Georgette said to her. "Is it a full flight?"

"Almost. Not quite."

"Okay, so is it possible that we could have this extra seat, then? Because if you're going to have to move me every time one of them wants out…"

The flight attendant made a face. "Right. Point taken. I'll see what I can do."

Georgette winked. "There you go. Move over and make yourself comfy."

Jess sighed, then moved over to the window and stretched her legs out over the middle seat.

"Just like a recliner," Georgette said.

"I'll take it."

Georgette opened her bag and took out a pair of earphones, leaning back in her seat as the rest of the passengers filed in.

CHAPTER SEVEN

The sun, high over her head, reminded Jil of why the hell she'd gotten out of icy, gray Rockland. She walked up the ramp and through the open gate, looking around for someone in a uniform. It was barely a mile walk, and after applying a good squirt of sunscreen and jamming on a baseball hat, she felt confident enough to jog to the place.

After all, with its blazing billboards and life-sized shark statues, the sea aquarium was probably visible from outer space.

Keeping the sign in sight, she ran with one ear bud in, stopping three times to drink water. By the time she got there, she was baking hot and had to pee. Shit, the sun was hot down here.

Jil strode out to the outdoor concrete sidewalk, spotting two trainers sitting on the boardwalk, making hand gestures to the dolphins and throwing fish.

She stood on the rampart and waved until one waved back uncertainly. She motioned that she'd like to come down, and the tall blond guy sprang up and loped over to her.

"Can I help you?"

"Hello, I'm Jil Kidd."

"Hi." He still looked uncertain.

"I'm looking for Rebecca Mason."

"Oh." He opened the gate and jogged up the stairs, then hopped the rampart and struck off for the entrance of the building she'd just come from.

"She's probably in the basement observing Tsunami."

Jil followed him through the doors and down the stairs to a lower observatory.

"Rebecca?"

"In here."

In the semi-darkness, Jil spotted a tall woman with dark auburn hair sitting on a stone bench. She faced toward a wall of safety glass, swaying gently to the classical music that played over the loudspeaker. An orca swam over to the far side of the tank, plunging down to the depths of the tank and back up.

Rebecca turned around and lifted her chin in greeting, then stood up slowly and approached Jil.

"I'm glad you're here," she said in a low voice, nearly whispering.

She guided Jil away from the observation glass and closer to the doorway. Jil wondered why they were whispering.

"Whales have very sensitive systems," Rebecca said, as if in answer to her question. "That's why we keep it dark down here. It deters people from quick movements."

"Does that also explain the Mozart?" Jil asked.

Rebecca half-smiled. "Good ear."

Jil thought of Jess's dinnertime playlists. Maybe she'd been educated more than she thought.

"Yes, to answer your question. It's hard to scream over classical."

Jil took in the signs posted around the area: *Please speak quietly. Do not tap glass.*

Rebecca followed her gaze. "We have a guard here when the park is open," she said. "If a whale got spooked and decided to ram the safety glass, we'd have a real problem."

"I think you've already got a pretty big problem, don't you?"

Rebecca stiffened beside her, then relaxed when she saw Jil's face—which she'd purposely kept neutral. "Why don't we go upstairs?"

"The whale show has been postponed indefinitely since the incident," Rebecca said, leading her up the concrete stairs, splashed with water, and into another wing. They traveled down a carpeted hallway to a back office.

"How many trainers do you have here?" Jil asked as they rounded the corner.

"Eight. Well, seven." She stopped at the door. "Seven now."

Jil took out her notebook and jotted that down. "I'd like to interview them."

"Of course. How long are you here for?"

"Just a week, if all goes well."

"Goes well…" Rebecca muttered. "I wonder what that would look like, exactly."

"Sorry," Jil said. "Bad choice of words, maybe."

"No, don't worry about it. I am hoping for a positive outcome here."

"What are you thinking happened?" Jil knew she probably shouldn't ask, as her job was to find out the truth, not what a client wanted to hear, but an owner of a facility paying her to find out if something wasn't an accident was highly unusual. Murder was far more damaging a problem to reconcile with the public than an accident.

"I don't believe Tsunami killed anyone," Rebecca said. "But if she did, I have no idea what I'd do. I can't afford to keep a whale that can't be trained, and nobody would buy her after this. My first responsibility is to my staff. Then my animals."

"Why did you purchase her in the first place if you knew she'd already rammed a trainer?"

Rebecca stopped and turned, surprised.

Jil leveled her gaze back.

"You do your homework, don't you?"

Jil waited.

"To answer your question, we were in negotiations for another whale. Unfortunately, the whale we were going to purchase died before we could have it transferred here. The other sea aquarium was filing for bankruptcy so we couldn't get our money back, but they sent us a female instead. A breeder. They said she was known to have caused problems, but I didn't have much choice at that point. Our tank was bigger and she'd have dolphins for company here. Either we took Tsunami or we'd be out almost half a million dollars."

Jil didn't respond. Seemed like losing half a million dollars might've been the better option...

Rebecca scanned her key card in front of a door, and it buzzed open.

They pushed their way into an office where a young guy was lounging on a hammock chair, a laptop on his chest.

"This is Leonard, my partner."

He smiled and sat up as much as he could in the hammock. As he maneuvered himself, Jil noticed he had a metal prosthetic from the left knee down.

"Silent, mostly," Leonard said. "I just do the accounting. Rebecca deals with people."

"He's being modest," Rebecca said. "He was quite an accomplished trainer, back in the day."

"Yeah, before that shark tried to eat me. Now I stick with numbers."

Leonard smiled awkwardly but shook her hand firmly, his too-large square glasses slipping down his nose. He pushed them up.

"I don't envy her at the moment," Leonard added.

"And I don't envy you," Rebecca replied.

Leonard sighed and stretched. His face was lined with stubble, like he'd been working too many long nights. "Without the revenue from the whale attraction, we're going to be sunk. I've tried to do a little creative accounting here to keep us afloat, but unless we get a resolution, soon, we're in trouble."

"I'm just going to fill Jil in on the details of that night. Unless you'd like to add anything."

Leonard shuddered. "No, thank you. I lived through it once and that's enough. I've got a date with the hot dog stand." He swung out of the hammock chair, his prosthetic smacking the floor with a thud.

Jil watched him go.

"How old was he when he lost his leg?"

"Seven."

Jil turned back.

"He lost it in a car wreck."

"But he said…"

"Oh, yes. He did get attacked by a shark here some years ago, but he'd already lost the leg when it happened. He had a good chunk of his upper arm taken out, but after a few surgeries, it looks all right." She shrugged. "Won't get back in the water, though. It's too bad. He was good at his job."

Rebecca picked up a box from her desk and plunked it down on the table in front of Jil.

"Here's everything I've put together for you. A file. A few videos. And the call to the police."

Jil sat down and began skimming through the information.

"I'm yours for the morning, so let's get started."

"Great." Jil flipped open her notebook. "Let's start with the roster of staff. Who works here, their dates of hire, and their employee files."

Rebecca searched out a pile on her desk and handed it to Jil.

"Is this everybody? Trainers, maintenance?"

"Everybody," Rebecca answered. "Even me."

"Thanks." She checked that off her list. "A record of the animals. A complete list of which animals are here now, when they came, where they came from, and who their main trainers are."

"Wow. Okay. That one may take some time."

"Okay. We can work on that today. Now, they all think I'm an accountant?"

"Yeah. I thought it was better for now."

"Right. So I'm going to hang around for a few days, not do any formal interviews, but see what I can get from just getting to know people a little better."

"Sounds good."

Jil looked at the staff list, then back at Rebecca, a question forming in her mind.

Then they heard screaming from outside.

Rebecca took off at a run down the hall, Jil following closely behind her.

Tait, the young trainer, was coming toward them up the ramp. "She's ramming the tank. It's gonna pop, Rebecca."

Rebecca ran faster—so fast Jil had a hard time keeping up to her.

"If that tank breeches, we're going to have a busted enclosure and a dead whale. We've got to stop her."

Jil imagined the crack in the glass of the viewing area spidering and splintering. The water surging through the opening, a giant waterfall into the underground viewing deck. And Rebecca was running straight into the fray.

"Do you really think you should go down there?"

"It's the best place to see her from," Rebecca called as she jogged down the stairs in her low-heeled pumps.

Jil followed and stopped at the sight of a giant whale head battering the glass. Leaks sprang from the bolts on one side.

"Fuck," Rebecca said.

She approached the glass and put up her arms as Tsunami charged again.

"This thing is going to breach."

Jil's heart thudded loudly. Would she make it to the stairs in time if the water started pouring in?

Rebecca flipped on the lights and turned up the music, making the serene underground sanctuary come alive like a disco. The whale stopped just short of the glass, and Rebecca breathed out a sigh of relief as she reached out to squeeze Jil's forearm. Her fingers were ice cold and shaky.

Her radio crackled and a man's voice hailed them.

"I've opened the barrier!" said Ramone.

"Good. Get out some food and bang the bucket. Let's get her the hell into the performance tank."

"Already on it. Almost ready."

"Well, do it quickly. This glass is about to breach."

From somewhere up above, Jil heard a sound like a crowbar striking metal.

Jil looked up, straight into the animal's wet, black eye. Tsunami looked at her steadily for a second and Jil held her hands up, backing away.

Tsunami slowly turned away and moved topside, her tail moving through the water with barely a bubble. Then she flipped and drove herself at the glass once more—a freight train colliding with the station.

One of the bolts popped and a stream of water burst like a fire hydrant cracking open. Jil felt a lurch of fear.

Another bolt popped, and another, sending water flooding into the observatory.

"Get that blowtorch up here, now!" Rebecca yelled into the radio.

She hadn't even finished speaking when Ramone came running down into the tank room, radio in one hand and a giant bag of equipment in the other.

"Get out of here, Rebecca. This thing could pop any second now."

Jil looked back up and the whale was gone.

"They're getting her into the performance tank. She'll have to stay there till we can get this fixed. However long that is."

Another bolt popped.

"The wall's buckling. We have to get it under control before the whole thing goes."

Rebecca's face had blanched.

"Where's maintenance?"

"They're afraid to come down here."

"Well, tell them to get over it. We need this tank fixed immediately!"

Ramone barked over the radio in Spanish, then French, and finally in a language Jil didn't recognize.

Within seconds, six young people were sprinting down the stairs, tossing equipment back and forth. The blowtorch lit up as they set to work, and Jil hoped that the animal was safely ensconced in whatever holding tank she'd been put into. This amount of noise and light would probably drive her crazy.

A clack on the stairs alerted her to Leonard entering the observatory. He stopped at the bottom of the stairwell, radio in hand.

"That animal is psychotic," he said quietly.

Rebecca turned around, her face drawn.

"We're going to have to accept it, Rebecca. I'm sorry. But the faster we unload that thing, the better for everyone."

"That may be true," Jil said. "I don't know much about whales, I'll give you that. But I do know that enclosure was tampered with."

Leonard stared at her. "Tampered with? Who the hell would be crazy enough to try to free Willy?"

Jil leaned down and picked up a bolt head that had been sawn off.

"Looks like someone else saw the movie…"

Leonard took it out of her hand and turned it slowly over in his fingers.

"Fuck."

A sound like a fire hydrant exploding sent them all barreling up the stairs.

"Go, go, go!" Rebecca yelled.

Leonard outstripped them, shouting into his radio. "Evacuate the observation deck. Evacuate the observation deck."

Rebecca collapsed on the outdoor bench seating.

"Fuck, what a mess," she said. "We need to get an industrial vacuum down here and some fans. Get this place dried out. And, Leonard, when that's done, call the police."

"You're sure you want to do that?" Leonard said doubtfully. "Remember what she was like the last time?"

Rebecca sighed. "Oh, how I wish I could handle this in-house. But we're in over our heads here. One death is enough for me. I can't afford a SeaWorld catastrophe. It might be time to cut our losses."

CHAPTER EIGHT

The chair, with its ripped arm and dented leg, still sat in the corner, almost reproaching Jess. How long had it been since she'd just sat here by Mitch's bedside? Talked to him? Visited for more than a few minutes, even?

Such a stark contrast to those first few weeks, when she'd done everything for him. The round-the-clock days when they waited to see if the swelling in his brain would go down, if he'd wake up.

Ironic, she'd touched him more in the first few months he'd been like this than in the last years of their marriage.

Rubbing cream into his heels, cracked and dry from the long winter. Stretching his legs, bending his knees until they almost touched his chest. At first, they'd been so heavy. So hard to maneuver. She'd lost her grip and let his leg crash to the bed once.

The surprise that his hair continued to grow as he lay still. The five o'clock shadow that crept over his cheeks. Shaving him.

Inevitable, but still unexpected—the ebb of life, creeping back in. One day she'd had to go home to wait for the plumber to come fix a leak…the next day, she'd finally conceded that she couldn't live on tea and peanut butter. She had to do the grocery shopping—alone, up and down the aisles of the indoor market— something she and Mitch had always done together. Saturday mornings. Fresh fish and an assortment of cheeses, soup bones, prime rib, oysters if they had them. The bakery for bread and cakes.

He loved to shop for food. To find new herbs and rub them between his fingers, letting her smell the earth and the pungent flavor she could infuse into their meals. He thrived on olives. And smoked meats. Artichoke hearts soaked in pickling juice, burrata smothered in top-notch olive oil and salt, spread on rosemary focaccia.

She loved to cook. He loved to eat.

She loved to garden. He loved the flowers erupting from vases all over the house.

Navigating the market alone. Carrying all the bags. Her hands and shoulders ached, and the doctor said it was probably just stress.

They didn't know then, of course. How difficult it would get. How many layers of alone she would feel over the next months.

After that first trip to the market, she put the food away and tried to imagine cooking for one. Tried to imagine the point of it.

How could she go back to the hospital when she had to catch up on bills, return the messages that had been piling up for the past five days, six, seven?

Two weeks, a month, and she went back to work. She had to—her leave was up. Her students needed her. Her bank account needed a paycheck.

Three months in, and she still visited in the evenings. Sat and read him the paper she used to read him during the morning visits she no longer had time for.

A weekend conference.

A dinner with friends.

Five months. Six.

Then she met Lily.

Jil.

Outside, freezing rain hit the windowsill, accreting on the glass until she could barely make out a dim glow of the streetlamps as they switched on in the dark early evening.

"Jessica, there you are."

Jess struggled out of her chair and shook hands with Dr. Rabinovitch. He leaned forward, his posture having deteriorated even more since she'd last seen him, so that he seemed to be permanently bent as if searching for something on the ground. His yarmulke had come slightly askew and was sitting at an odd angle on his head. He smiled wanly, but his drooping eyelids betrayed his weariness.

"Sorry to call you away from your holiday, Jessica."

Jess turned to Mitch.

"He looks so old, doesn't he?"

Dr. Rabinovitch sighed. "He's been in this state a long time. It's hard on your body, immobility."

Jess clasped his hand. "I've been sitting here with him, thinking about how he used to look. How tan he was. How strong."

Nothing in the wasted body before her resembled her husband anymore.

"What is that smell, Doctor?"

Two nurses swung in the door, one with an IV bag in hand.

They watched her hang it and change out the old one before the two of them set to work turning Mitch over.

Dr. Rabinovitch gently pulled her out of the way.

Jess swallowed hard.

"We're doing the best we can with rotating him every thirty minutes, but his skin is so broken down that it's hard to find a good spot. That bedsore on his buttock is seeping constantly. That's what you're smelling."

"Oh my God," Jess said, putting her hand to her throat.

"Unfortunately, that's not the worst of it. He does have septicemia."

Three heel clicks on the hallway floor was all it took for Jess's fingers to run cold.

Before she could even consider an escape route, the door swung open and Myra's eyes locked with hers.

For a moment, they stood staring at one another, Myra lifting her chin and breathing deeply through her nose, nearly a snort.

"Jessica," she said finally.

Jess desperately wanted to sit down, but wouldn't concede defeat so early in this round.

"Myra. I'm surprised to see you here."

It was exactly the wrong thing to say, of course. "Really? Because I've been here several times a week for the past five years. You. Have not."

You're also a retired old battle-ax with nothing else to do but sit in a hospital room, knitting and telling everyone how to do their jobs.

Which she did not say.

"How is my son today, Doctor?"

Dr. Rabinovitch sighed audibly. "No improvement, I'm afraid, Mrs. Blake."

She smiled as if he'd told her Mitch had made a full recovery overnight. "Well, my prayer circle will be here later this morning. I'm sure he'll be himself again in no time."

Myra looked at her again. "Would you mind, Jessica? I'd like some time alone with my son."

Jess stared at her. She was tempted to just walk out. Leave her to the lunacy that had sustained her all this time. But she couldn't this time.

She took a deep breath. "Actually, we were just discussing his final directives," she said.

Myra drew herself up, cold fury in her eyes. She sputtered before finally getting out the words. "His final directive is in God's hands. Not yours."

Jessica was tired of this argument. She'd been tired of it for years, but seeing Mitch's condition—smelling it, actually—was the deciding factor.

She closed the gap between them. She stood close so Myra could see the intent in her eyes. "I will be signing his DNR, Myra. It's time."

Her face drained white. "How dare you? How dare you come in here and pretend to be his next of kin?"

Jess reeled. She wasn't wrong. "I am his next of kin. I am his wife."

"Hardly. Hardly!"

Dr. Rabinovitch took her elbow and guided her to the door. Myra fluttered over Mitch and ran her hands over his face while the doctor led Jessica outside.

She sat down, shaking.

"Can I get you some water?"

She shook her head. "No. Thank you."

"Maybe we'd better organize a meeting," he suggested gently.

Jess laughed bitterly. "What's the point? She hasn't seen reason for the past five years. Why would she begin now?"

"His condition will only deteriorate," Dr. Rabinovitch said. "It will stop his heart. The only question is, how should we proceed when it does…?"

At home, on the porch, Jess lit the outdoor fireplace and tucked her feet up under the blanket. A book lay in her lap, but she couldn't bring herself to pick it up. Instead, she scrolled through Jil's latest text messages.

Skype at 6pm?

Still another ten minutes to wait.

She sat and looked out over the street. She sipped her wine and remembered the last time she and Mitch had sat here, side by side on this porch.

She imagined Myra, bible in one hand and crucifix in the other, rocking in the same chair by the window that Jess had been in for the first month after Mitch's accident. The same rocking chair she'd occupied after they'd told her he probably wouldn't wake up. Where she'd read the forms, read them again, and ultimately decided to take him off life support.

But Myra had wept so much, pleaded with her, that she'd changed her mind. She thought she was just allowing him to die naturally. She'd never imagined it would go on for five years. Five years.

Or that Myra's bitterness against her would blossom into something resembling hatred.

In sickness and in health. For better or for worse. You don't deserve to be his wife. He would never have left your side.

She sipped her wine and rocked.

At five to six, her tablet began to bleep. Quickly, she set down her wine and picked it up.

Jil's face swam into view. Or rather, her chin.

"Hold the phone away a little," Jess said.

Jil stretched it out. "Is that better? Fucking technology."

"Well, at least I can see your smiling face," Jess said wryly.

"Sorry."

Jil moved the phone and gave Jess a good view of her left nostril. "How are things going?"

Jess sighed and leaned back in her chair. "Terrible, as expected. You?"

"Well, I was almost killed by a whale today."

"What?"

"I jest. Sort of."

"Be careful, would you? I don't think I can manage the death of two spouses at once."

Jil pulled the phone away so she was looking right at Jess. "I wish I was there."

Jess sighed. "I do too. Actually, I wish I was there. I wish I had something to do other than think and stew."

"Well, I'm happy to send you my research!" Jil said brightly. "The Wi-Fi here is not great."

"I'll make you a deal. You take on Myra's prayer group and I'll do whatever field research you need."

"Sounds like a great trade," Jil said sarcastically. "She's still not backing down?"

"No. In fact, she's digging in her heels even more."

Jil leaned forward, squinting at the swing Jess sat on. "Wait, are you at your house?"

"Yeah. I didn't feel like being at your place without you."

"Our place."

Jess chuckled. "Your place. Where you pay the rent."

"Our place. Where you buy the groceries. You've been back to your place, what? Three nights in the past year?"

Jess shrugged. "Maybe four."

"You could just put it on the market, you know," Jil said softly.

Jess's stomach dropped. What would Myra say about *that?* Mitch was dying and she was rushing him into his grave by selling the house. But Jil had a point—being here alone wasn't any better than being at the loft alone. Maybe she should have checked into a hotel.

"I've just been waiting. You know, until he actually died. It's his house too…" her voice trailed off.

"Yeah. I understand."

But Jess got the feeling she didn't, really. She wiped her nose and changed the topic. "Hey, I saw Zeus out for a walk today. He gave me a big slobber."

Jil laughed. "Is he behaving himself?"

"Mostly, apart from an incident with a bathrobe…"

"Oh, wonderful. I'll expect a big bill in damages when I return."

"Sorry I can't go get him. It's just that the hours at the hospital are long."

"Don't worry," Jil said quickly. "He's fine. We'll get him as soon as I get home and then we'll all go back to our place together."

"Our place that's about to get sold?"

Jil sighed. "Don't remind me."

After they hung up, Jess swung for a long time, thinking. She would get a good amount of capital from this place. Enough to buy half the loft, if Jil wanted to stay there. Or they could get something else. A single-level, possibly…because she would need it. Soon. Two lesbians and a Great Dane. Maybe a few chickens and an alpaca.

The thought made her smile.

CHAPTER NINE

Jil followed Rebecca back to the office and sat down as Rebecca set to work on the coffee machine and leaned against the counter while she waited for it to brew.

"I understand if you want to go home for the day. That was a bit freaky, even for me."

Jil shrugged. "It's just me and an empty hotel room. I think I might get more done by observing what goes on in here."

"As long as the place doesn't go down like the *Titanic*."

Rebecca opened a tin and offered Jil a pastry. Macarons.

Why not? High calorie pastries seemed to be the way of life here.

"There's an amazing bakery up the beach. Probably half the reason I decided to stay on St. Emeline to start with."

Jil laughed. "I think I had their *pain au chocolat* this morning."

Rebecca smiled.

"So what made you decide to take the leap?"

The coffee machine drizzled out the last of the coffee, and Rebecca poured it into mugs. She smiled wanly. "Love."

"Oh? What happened?"

With a sigh, Rebecca settled back in her chair. "You really want to know?"

"Of course. I'm a PI. I run on coffee and curiosity."

Rebecca laughed. "Okay, well, there was this girl."

Jil grinned. "A gay girl or a straight girl?"

"Oh, she was most definitely a gay girl."

"And?"

"I met her here on a training seminar. We...hit it off."

"Meaning you U-Hauled?"

"Oh boy, did we ever. I sent home for my stuff and moved in with her. Never went home."

"And then?"

"Let's just say it ended badly."

"Does she still live here?"

"Sure does." Rebecca smiled tightly. "You? How's your girlfriend enjoying St. Emeline?"

Jil made a face. "Actually, she's back in Canada."

"What? You just got here."

Jil nodded. "Yup. She had to go home. Family emergency."

"Too bad."

"Yeah. Solo tropical vacation. Joy."

"Shitty."

"Thanks," Jil said. "So who has a vendetta against your whale? Or against you?"

Rebecca looked at her quizzically. "Against me? I have no idea. It's my trainer who was killed."

"Yes, but your tank that was sabotaged. And your sea aquarium that's paying the price. Not to mention it's you that has to handle a potential murder investigation."

"So you do think it's possible it wasn't Tsunami?"

Jil tilted her head. "It's not my job to have an opinion. You asked me to investigate the possibility and I am. But if the whale didn't kill that girl, then the next most likely suspect is a person. Which means someone you know."

Rebecca bit her lip. "Right."

"And not only someone you know, Rebecca, but someone you see every day."

"Jesus."

"Exactly."

Leonard popped his head in the door. "Police are here."

"Shit," she muttered.

Jil peered out the front window.

A group of small white cars, checkered in yellow and blue, pulled into the cul-de-sac, lights on. Max was carrying a bucket of fish past the front door. He spotted the police cars and stopped, then turned back the way he came. She watched him go at a quick pace.

Was he just annoyed with the gendarme interrupting his workday, or was there another reason he was avoiding the police?

Jil turned to follow him, but he disappeared before she could see where he went. She turned around just as the troupe came marching out of the main building, Rebecca leading the way to Tsunami's temporary tank. A woman with short brown hair marched half a pace behind her. Her cap sat rigidly on her head and was white where the others were blue. Presumably, she was the captain. And by the way she was glowering at Rebecca, it seemed that they knew each other.

"I assume there's a good reason we still have a whale problem here. Why is this animal not in an enclosure?"

"She was," Rebecca said tensely. "She tried to break out of it. So we put her in the outdoor pool."

"Where anyone can just jump the fence and try to pet her, I suppose?" Her accent was heavily laced with French, and Jil had the distinct impression that speaking English was an added annoyance for her.

"I don't see a whole lot of people here, do you, Inspector?"

"Perhaps you should just show me to the site. Assuming I'm not going to be attacked and eaten down there."

Rebecca rolled her eyes. "Come with me, please."

The inspector beckoned to her deputy, and he followed her out, a camera in hand. They had to shout to be heard over the noise of the industrial vacuum, which had all but finished clearing out the water from the observation deck.

"What makes you think this tank was tampered with?" the inspector said tersely.

"Three bolts popped along one side. That's almost impossible."

"Could it not be that the facility is just getting old, Ms. Mason? That this glass, as lovely as it is, was not designed for a five-ton animal to ram its body weight against it?"

Rebecca took a deep breath.

"Obviously, it was not designed for that purpose, Carole. But the possibility was taken into account. It shouldn't have breeched like this."

"Maybe you should take it as a divine signal from the universe, Rebecca. Frankly, I'm surprised you're still open. I'd think the insurance payments alone would sink you."

"We're still just trying to figure out what happened."

"What happened is you have a facility that's falling down and undertrained staff who don't know enough to stay away from killer whales after hours."

"I think it's more than that."

"You have no evidence!"

"No, you have no evidence because you refuse to look!"

The inspector threw her arms up. "Do you think we have unlimited resources? Money, time, officers? We investigated. The medical report was clear. End of topic. Now, if you want me to open an investigation on vandalism, I will be happy to do that."

Jil sidled up to the tank to hear better.

"Yes," Rebecca answered.

"Yes?"

"Yes. Yes I want you to investigate the vandalism."

"Fine."

The captain turned and stared at Jil. "I don't believe we've met. New friend of yours, Rebecca?"

Jil smiled tensely. "I'm just visiting."

The captain looked at her warily. "You've picked an interesting time."

"I'm getting some independent tax advice, if you must know," Rebecca said.

"Do what you need to do, Rebecca. Spend your money however you like, but let me make it clear: if there is another incident here, we will be citing you with criminal charges."

Rebecca pulled her aside. "I am trying my best here, Carole."

"And your best seems to involve keeping this whale at the potential loss of human life. You have a dead trainer being towed around this basin by a murderous killer whale who's now almost flooded your observation deck. What if someone else had been killed? What other proof do you need?"

"I know you're looking for a speedy answer here."

"I'm looking to keep the people on this island safe!"

"Fine. I know. But I have other responsibilities."

"If it were up to me, this place would be shut down and you would be on the first plane back to Canada."

Jil winced. Wow.

Rebecca didn't flinch. Instead, she sighed.

"I'm aware. And yet, I called you."

"Well, you have my input."

With that, the inspector turned and marched out, taking her contingent with her.

Rebecca sighed and leaned against the wall. "Well, that was pleasant."

"Past lover?" Jil guessed.

"How did you know?"

"Nobody but a woman scorned has venom like that."

Rebecca looked up, over the lagoon.

"Wait. She was the one?"

Rebecca nodded. "It was good for a while, but you know how things go…"

"So that's what's clouding her judgment? She's not over the breakup?"

"Guess she has the right," Rebecca confessed. "I kinda… slept with someone else."

"Oh."

"I'm probably not the world's most faithful lover."

Jil didn't answer. She knew that temptation a little too well.

"She wants me off the island and out of her life. But I can't just pack up shop as easily as that. Even if she does have the right to be here. This is her home, not mine…"

"Well. I guess it's yours now too. We'll just have to see what we can do about keeping it that way."

Rebecca laid a hand on Jil's forearm. "Thank you for coming. They're blind when it comes to this."

Jil felt a surprising jolt at Rebecca's touch, but didn't move her arm.

"You're right to be suspicious," she said. "And I intend to find out exactly what happened here."

CHAPTER TEN

Jess almost hadn't left the hospital, but the nurses had insisted she get some rest. Her own health was suffering, and she knew she had to take care or risk making herself worse. But every red light gave her an opportunity to start thinking again. Remembering.

It had been five years and she'd rebuilt her life. Met someone else. She'd never expected to be deluged with these memories that were so physical. Almost like she was standing inside them, watching them play out.

His hand along the back of her neck. Down her shoulder.

The move away from him was almost involuntary. A dip, a twitch, a slight pulling up of her shoulder. Like brushing off a fly landing.

He moved his hand.

"I need you, Jess. I'm dying here."

He was so close she could feel him against her—hard, impatient.

Tears sprang to her eyes, strangling her voice even more, even if she could have spoken. Even if she could have found words to tell him—to explain this wall, this ever growing layer between them.

She moved away. Picked up the car keys.

Groceries and the bank and school. Her ever-demanding students. Her teachers. Most of the time she was so busy she couldn't think.

"No. You have to talk to me this time. Stop running away from me."

He grabbed her wrist and she froze.

She could just jerk him off in the shower and he'd leave her alone.

That's how it had been for years.

But now…now, she couldn't bring herself to touch him, even for the sake of peace.

"Please, Jessie."

She looked away, breathed through the way he held her wrist. Didn't pull away. Didn't force him to let her go. Because what would that mean? What would it say if he didn't?

His breath on her neck shot down her spine as he pressed his nose to the back of her head.

"It's been months, Jess. God."

Close to a year, actually. But—

He tensed, and she braced herself for his anger. His frustration with her silence and her withdrawal. With the way she turned away from him and snapped the light off.

Would he ever force her, if it came right down to it?

"What's happened to us? Do you not love me at all?" His voice broke.

Not what she'd expected. Mitch never broke down.

She didn't look up to see the tears she knew were glassing his eyes.

His grip on her wrist tightened for a second, and then he let her go.

"What have I done to you to deserve this?"

He shoved away from her and stormed off toward the bathroom.

Slammed the door.

She heard the rustling of magazine pages. The unzipping. The grunts and moans he made no attempt to silence.

She could see it all so clearly—the way his face looked when he made that sound, when he was close to coming and he grabbed her hair or her shoulder and pushed into her.

The way she used to like it because it made her feel powerful. Even if she never came until later, alone, after he'd fallen asleep, when she touched herself.

He'd tried; she had to give him that, in the beginning when they were first married. She'd never let him go down on her—the thought of it made her cringe—but he'd turn her over and cup her breasts in one hand, slide the other between her legs and touch her gently, then more firmly, harder, until she came, moaning into the pillow.

He used to have the patience for the orgasms that built for half an hour before quietly imploding, yielding to the friction of his fingers in the dark, making her entire body tingle.

When they had time to do it in the morning or on the weekend afternoons. When she wanted to open up to him, wanted to love him like that.

The toilet flushed.

The door opened.

He tucked in his shirt. Shook his head at her as he walked out the door.

She took a deep breath, the look on his face making it hard to swallow. The sound of him coming still gave her a shiver in the pit of her stomach—the primal groan, the shuddering breath and gasp.

But the thought of him touching her made her want to cry.

For a moment after the door closed, she felt like his hand was on her stomach, twisting her. She didn't even feel the tears starting, but suddenly she was sobbing. Sitting on the kitchen floor, back to the cupboards, tears splashing onto her chest, hot and furious.

What had happened to them? Why?

Was it just that she was tired? Or not interested? Or did she really not love him anymore?

She sat longer than she should have. Long enough that she'd sit in traffic an extra twenty minutes, and wouldn't have time to stop for a latte, but Mitch's face as he walked through the door... The way he didn't stop to kiss her, even though he always stopped—always. Even if they'd been fighting. Even if she wanted to hit him and he knew it.

He always stopped to kiss her.

The new teacher orientation and dinner kept her late, and by the time she got in past ten, Mitch was already asleep. She picked up his orange hunting vest that lay on the floor where it had dropped off the side of the couch and replaced it on top of his bag. Mitch and the guys would be gone all weekend, and she was equal parts relieved to have the house to herself and guilt ridden for feeling that way.

Forty-eight hours to garden and go on nature hikes. Feel the grass, smell the changing leaves. The thought of strolling alone up the stone trail behind her house physically relaxed her. She felt the muscles in her back unclench. Alone. Peaceful. Without the weight of this hand in her hand that was growing increasingly heavy and unfamiliar.

What was wrong with her?

He wasn't a bad man.

He was kind. Funny. Respectful. A role model to so many students. A good principal. She'd learned a lot from him.

But she didn't love him, and that thought weighed more heavily on her than any look of reproach he could give.

For him, divorce wasn't an option. But it had been on her mind daily for the last year. Or was it two?

She didn't hear him get up. The open window and the glass of wine she'd sipped at the orientation had given her an unusual full night's sleep. His alarm had been set for five—no wonder she hadn't heard him.

Had he kissed her head while she slept? Or had he just picked up and left?

She glanced at the clock: 7:46. By now he'd be there. Loading up the ATVs, probably.

Funny how she knew exactly what he'd be up to, even though she'd never been on one of these expeditions. He'd been at it for as long as she'd known him.

It had been just like this—half a dozen messages on a phone she was too busy to answer or hadn't heard ring. A long, adrenaline-fueled trip to the hospital—this hospital. Days and nights sitting up in a chair—this chair.

Meeting with the doctors, the surgeons, the nurses. And later the police. His friends. Dropping by for the first few days, then never again.

His students sending cards. And then offering Mass. A prayer included at every school function, like a ritual, a nod to the favorite teacher who'd spend the rest of his life in a hospital bed.

CHAPTER ELEVEN

Jil had spent the past two days locked in Rebecca's office, going over video footage of the night Tasha had been killed. The dark night, coupled with the fact that some of the video cameras were not functioning—and the one that *was* working was angled the wrong way—made it nearly impossible to establish any reliable account.

Still, she'd managed to track the comings and goings of most of the staff on video, and had narrowed down the list of people present at the aquarium that night to three: Rebecca, who'd left for home at her usual time; Ramone, who'd shown up on one of the cameras in the back halls around 7:00 that night; and a male trainer she couldn't identify. Only the back of his head made a brief appearance on camera as he rounded a corner, and it wasn't possible to tell hair color or anything else on the black and white footage.

Rebecca was out for the day meeting with lawyers, so she made a note of Ramone's activity and kept watching. Tasha had been killed sometime after dark, which, at this time of year, meant anytime after 7:15.

At lunch, she stretched and her stomach growled, reminding her that she hadn't eaten since six.

She let herself out of the office and went in search of the hotdog stand—the only source of food in the park, unless you brown-bagged it, which she had no intention of doing.

"How's your tax appraisal going?" Ramone asked, squirting ketchup on a hotdog as she approached.

Jil shrugged. "Not bad. One, please," she said to the vendor.

He turned and handed her a jumbo-sized dog.

"What's good?" she asked Ramone.

He smiled around a bite of hotdog. "Corn relish. Or straight ketchup. Whatever you like."

Jil laughed. "I was hoping for iguana paste or something we didn't have at home."

Ramone shook his head. "Naw. Though I guess you only have frozen hot dogs in your *neck of the woods*, eh?"

She fixed him with a look. The man's love of idioms was hilarious. "You know we do have four seasons, right? Only half of them are winter."

He laughed and sat on a bench overlooking the dolphin training lagoon.

"Canadian government must have some pretty strict rules to make it worth Rebecca's money to fly you out here."

"I'm worth my fee," Jil said, winking. "Though things are certainly a lot more complicated with this…incident."

"Incident. More like a nightmare," Ramone said. "My own kid used to feed that whale. Imagine if something had happened to him. Imagine if she'd snatched him from the side."

He looked genuinely upset.

"Is that why you don't let him come around anymore?"

Ramone nodded. "He's too curious. Could get hurt."

"Where's his mother?" Jil asked.

"At work. We're all at work. Me, my wife, my two oldest. Even my mother. But Abuela can work and watch Emi at the same time. He's in school, but only half days, right? Used to bring him with me, but not no more."

"Were you here the night she was killed?" Jil asked.

Ramone gave her a strange look. Then he shook his head. "No. I leave at five every night, after my shift."

Jil looked at him and nodded. But she'd seen him on camera. Why was he lying? She couldn't ask without blowing her cover.

Ramone shuddered. "What a disaster."

Jil stayed silent for a few moments. Ramone was lost in thought.

"How did they get her out of the tank?" she asked.

"Next morning, early," Ramone said. "When the first staff came in and we found her."

"She wasn't found until the next day?"

"She'd been in the water all night. The pool was red. Her body was all bloated... Never mind."

He looked sick.

Jil just waited. He didn't seem like he needed any prompting. Obviously, this night was weighing on his conscience—whatever the reason.

"Tsunami was carrying her around the pool."

Jil was surprised. That hadn't been in the case notes. "Carrying her?"

"Something orcas do sometimes."

"In her mouth?"

"No, on her nose. Holding her above the water, swimming round and round the tank. At first we didn't know what to do. We could tell she was dead, of course, but we didn't know how to get her out. We called the police. Called Rebecca. We tried to get Tsunami into a different tank so the rescue workers could get to Tasha's body, but...it was an effort."

"How so?"

"Well, Tsunami was agitated. She wasn't listening to commands, and everyone was on edge. Finally, Leonard come and got her to move. He baited her with something—a salmon, I think, and she moved away. Baz was a wreck. Max was crying, even. It was terrible."

"Why was she here?" Jil asked.

"I don't know. I've been trying to figure that out ever since it happened. What was Tasha doing here at that time of night? Why did she come back?"

Jil studied his body language. He seemed truthful—genuinely distraught and confused—but he was still lying. He had been here that night. What had he seen? Or done?

"Any clues?"

He shook his head. "Baz said they had a date but she didn't show up."

"But you don't believe him?"

Ramone got up. "I have no reason not to believe him," he said. "They were a cute couple. Now, let's make this long story short. We have animals to feed, right?"

Jil stared after him as he left, more confused now than she'd been before.

CHAPTER TWELVE

Young men attending Friday morning confessions always amused Jess. Good Catholics getting ready to purge their sins before a weekend of random sex and binge drinking. Maybe she was getting cynical in her old age, or maybe it was the fact that she knew teenage boys better than their own mothers did—years of teaching high school ingrained memories she'd rather have forgotten—images she could never get out of her head.

So when the young man held the door for her, she smiled at him. Good for you for at least making an effort, she thought. He looked like a college student. First in line for the confessional, ducking in just before the time began.

She took off her coat and laid it in a pew, then made the sign of the cross and slipped into a kneeling position. A borrowed rosary would have to do. As she ran the white plastic beads between her fingers, she wondered how many babies had sucked on it during Mass, using it as a pacifier.

The door opened and closed behind her, and footsteps sounded to her left. She looked up, wondering if Father McGillivray was on his way into the confessional.

Someone stood beside her and she looked up. The young man from the doorway smiled down at her, wearing a black shirt and a clerical collar.

"Really?" she said before she could stop herself.

He grinned. "I'm new here."

"I can see that."

"Are you here for Confession?"

"Well, yes, but, Father…"

The name felt strange on her tongue. How old was this kid? He had to be older than he looked to have had time to get through seminary.

"Something else?"

"Well, generally, it's supposed to be anonymous."

He chuckled. "I'd already seen you, so I thought I might as well introduce myself. I'm Gus Makarios."

"Father Makarios?"

"Father Gus, around here. Makarios seems a bit hard for the kids."

"Well, welcome."

Jess struggled to get onto the pew, and Father Gus held out a hand. With a surprisingly strong grip, he helped her from kneeling to sitting.

"Thanks," she muttered.

He slid into the pew beside her. "Since there's nobody else here," he said, gesturing to the empty room. He reached down to put the kneeler back up and retrieve Jess's fallen rosary.

She leaned back in the pew and crossed her legs at the ankle. "Thanks for that as well."

He looked at her. "What if we have a conversation instead of a confession?" he suggested.

"I don't even think I'd know where to start."

"Would you prefer the more traditional approach?"

She thought for a second. Listing her sins:

Impure thoughts.

Adultery.

And if she pulled the plug…manslaughter?

"I don't know what I have to confess, Father." She realized as she spoke that this was what had been holding her back from

Confession. This very reluctance to call what she and Jil had built a sin at all. To frame it in a way that needed an apology and divine forgiveness. She couldn't go to Mass and sleep with Jil every night, but she refused to confess to a life. A partnership.

"My husband is dying," she said instead.

Father Gus looked at her with concern. "I'm so sorry to hear that. You've very young, so I imagine he is too."

"He is forty." Forty. God, when had that happened? They'd gone out on that trip to celebrate his thirty-fifth birthday. He'd left that morning.

She'd gone to the bakery on her lunch hour to pick up his cake.

That night, she'd received the call.

And that cake had stayed in the fridge a week before she'd thrown it out.

Forty. How could he be forty? He hadn't lived for the past five years.

"Jessica?"

She realized she was staring at nothing. "Time's gone on, Father. Without him. I know that. I've been living without him for five years. But it's just a shocking thing to think about, suddenly. He's forty years old."

"Your husband, Mitch Blake, am I right?"

"Yes, Father." She wasn't surprised he knew Mitch's name. The students at his school still had Mass said for him at least twice a year.

"It's been five years, you say, since his accident?"

"Yes. He's developed septicemia from a bed sore. His organs are toxic."

"He's dying," Father Gus finished.

"Imminently," Jess said. "But slowly. And painfully, I'm afraid. I don't know. I agreed to all the drugs, all the pain management, but I don't know how much pain he's in. I don't know how much he's suffered lying unconscious."

"And you are struggling with his death now?"

"I'm struggling with the fact that the doctors have just as well as told me to pull the plug."

Father Gus leaned forward, resting his hands on the back of the pew in front. "I see."

"Do you?"

"I see why that would be a struggle, yes. On one hand, you don't want to prolong his suffering; on the other, you don't want to cause his death."

"I haven't got a right to either," Jess said. "And I think I've lost the right to make decisions for him. I'm no longer sure I'd know exactly what he'd say. What he'd want. But his mother… his mother is adamant that we do nothing."

Father Gus tilted his head from side to side, as if physically weighing options. "Well, it seems to me that both choices are in the hands of others as well as you. God Himself will play the final role, don't you think?"

"Yes, probably," Jess said. "But I wish He'd hurry up."

"God's timing…" he said softly.

"Has never been mine." She smiled ruefully.

"What if it is his time now? What if God is calling him home, and you only have to let him go?"

She stared at him. "If it were me, I would have wanted it to end a long time ago," she said.

"You would have refused extraordinary measures?"

"I would have, yes."

"So why did you not refuse for him?" His open, frank way of speaking made her feel like telling him everything.

She breathed out hard, blowing the hair out of her eyes. "I didn't even consider it at the time. Letting him go. He was so young. His accident was so sudden, and the doctors weren't sure whether the damage was permanent. There were so many uncertainties. They said they were going to stick him on that machine, and I said fine."

"And now?"

"Now, he's dying. He's septic. The smell, Father." Her voice caught.

"And what is it you're afraid of?"

His insight was remarkable. He seemed so much older than he looked.

"Not his death in itself…"

"No." She breathed out. "I'm afraid that his death would uncomplicate my life."

"That you'd be free to move on?"

"Yes."

"To find happiness?"

"Yes."

"And you're afraid that your desire for freedom is impacting your decision to let Mitch go?"

She nodded.

He frowned for a second, looking out over the pews.

"I wonder—what if this is your release as well as Mitch's? What if this is Mitch's call home, and your call to the rest of your life?"

"I guess this is where we list my adultery?"

Father Gus nodded. "Seems like a good time, yes."

"With another woman?"

Was she trying to shock him on purpose? See how far she could push this liberal young priest before the understanding in his eyes clouded over and he decided that she really should have been in the confessional from the start?

He leaned forward, his smile turning into a look of concern. "I see. Ever more complicated."

"Any time you want to stop listening, Father."

He looked at her. "Why would I want to stop listening? You are a member of my parish and you are in need of council. Please talk as long as you like. What's the name of your partner?"

"Jil," she said, a little surprised.

"You met Jil where?"

Jess thought back to the very first day she'd met Jil Kidd—undercover in her school. She hadn't even known her real name back then.

"At work," she said.

Father Gus looked at her, as though he wanted to ask something else. "There's probably more to that story, but we'll come back to it if you feel like it," he suggested.

"Probably a good idea, yes."

A memory had taken firm hold...of Jil pushing her against a wall, slipping a very skilled hand down the front of her pants...

She felt herself blushing and purposely turned her gaze to a mural on the wall until the flush could leave her cheeks. She smiled up at Father Gus benignly.

"Were you from a very open seminary?" she asked before he could turn the conversation back to her.

He shrugged. "Not really, no. But I was raised by two mothers."

"Really?" She couldn't hide her surprise.

He laughed. "Yep, that's usually the reaction I get. Except that you seem more pleased-and-surprised than shocked-and-surprised."

"I am definitely both pleased and surprised. How did you decide to become a priest?"

"My mothers weren't Catholic, actually, but they accepted my call to God, even if they didn't understand it."

Jess tried to imagine that. How she and Jil would raise a child—have him baptized, bring him to church. She couldn't.

"Well, you are certainly an interesting person, Father Gus."

"As are you, Ms. Blake."

"I think I've done enough confessing for today."

"We have certainly covered a lot of ground."

She smiled, waiting.

He seemed to suddenly catch on to why she was sitting there still.

"Would it make you feel better to have penance?"

Wasn't that why people usually came to Confession? To undergo the illusion of atonement? Prayers washed the soul clean, didn't they?

"It would, probably. Because Mitch was old-fashioned."

"Not because you are?" He smiled.

She stopped. She'd never considered herself particularly traditional. "Maybe a little. Catholic school principal and all that."

"I'd say it was definitely a trapping of your line of work."

She bowed as he made the sign of the cross over her head and absolved her of sins she hadn't actually confessed. Still, the tears that slid down her cheeks felt healing.

"I think you need more counseling than confessing," Father Gus said quietly.

She pulled her purse closer to her and made to stand up. "I think you may be right, Father."

He stood up first and helped her out into the aisle, where she turned to the altar and made the sign of the cross from a standing position.

"Forgive me if I don't genuflect."

Father Gus shook his head. "Not at all. 'Stand and kneel as you are able.'"

"Ah. Unitarian," she said, a smile stretching her face.

His eyes widened. "Yes. My mother was Unitarian. How did you know?"

"They're the only ones I've ever heard use that expression."

"Yes, well, we're about to integrate it here. Are you coming to Mass on Sunday?"

She considered. "I might, you know. I just might."

"Good. And if you can't make it, why don't you meet me back here during Monday Confession?"

Jess smiled and turned toward the door. "Thank you. I will."

Chapter Thirteen

Jil walked along the outer wall that overlooked the dolphins' lagoon. Spray from the breaking waves doused her face, which had gotten too much sun yesterday and still ached from the sunburn.

Rebecca joined her, hitching herself up onto the wall.

"How's it going?"

Jil frowned. "Well, I've talked to almost everyone, but I've hit a bit of a roadblock."

"Anything you're ready to share?"

"No." Jil had a strict policy about sharing anything before a final report.

"Well, I think you've earned a little recreation, don't you?"

Jil looked at her.

"Such as?"

Rebecca winked. "Ever swum with dolphins before?"

Jil shook her head.

"Nothing like getting your feet wet!"

"I've never been within chomping distance, and I'd like to keep it that way."

With a snort, Rebecca gestured to the lagoon. "I don't think there's been a dolphin attacking a human in recorded history. Like, ever."

"There's always a first time."

Rebecca rolled her eyes. "Wow. All right. You can do the open water exercise tomorrow."

"You take the dolphins into the ocean? Don't they swim away?"

Rebecca shook her head. "Nope. This is their home and their family. They're a pod and they like to be together. Every day, they get to go out and play. We take out a motor boat and guide them around, but they always follow us back."

"That's some trust."

"Well, for a lot of the dolphins, this is the only home they've known. Three of them were born here. And they do important work. That's why I want to keep this place open. If I had to close, who knows what would happen to them?" She looked tired all of a sudden.

"What work do they do?"

"Wait and see. You'll find out. Just suit up and head on down to the back forty."

Jil felt her heart thudding. "Great."

She emerged from the locker area, her slightly damp suit making her skin crawl. Why had she agreed to this?

She stood by the wall, overhearing voices from below. She crept forward a bit and listened.

"Slammed, man. Covering all of Baz's shifts."

"Why?"

"Need the money. Girlfriend lost her job and we're locked into our lease. Otherwise I'd move."

"You've got a nice place."

"Yeah, definitely. Love the water and whatever, but it's tight right now."

"Heard from Baz?"

"Naw. Not since he gave his two weeks'. Can't blame him."

"No shit. You wouldn't stick around a place where your girlfriend was killed either."

"Damn straight. I'd leave the island. Vanessa's my life. Another reason I need the money. Saving for a ring."

His buddy shoved him. "No way! You're gonna tie the noose?"

"Sunset wedding. The whole shebang. Sure am. Life's too short, man."

"Ha ha. Tait the Great's gonna be a married man. Yeah. I get that. Hey, good for you."

"Thanks. What about you? Seeing anyone special?"

But his buddy didn't laugh. Instead he just mumbled something about, "Not anyone you know," and turned away.

Jil emerged from the doorway.

"Hey."

The two guys looked up, and then down at their feet.

"Hey," said the blond one.

"I'm Jil."

"Yeah. You're doing a dolphin experience?"

Jil smiled. "I'm hoping it's not a drowning experience."

The guy with the mop of dark hair gave her a grin. "I'm Max. This is Tait."

"Hi, guys."

"You're visiting Rebecca?"

"Yeah. Tax appraisal." Jil wondered if there was anything in the world she'd be less suited to than her cover job.

"She's buttering you up?" Tait winked.

"Could be. Why? Something I should know?"

She'd meant to be light, but they both clammed up right away, looking back at the ground.

"Joking, guys."

Max nodded. "Let's get you into the water."

She followed him down and he handed her a pair of flippers. "First thing you've got to do is get used to the flippers and mask. We'll just get into the water for a bit, without the dolphins."

"Sounds good."

She would have been perfectly happy to avoid the dolphins altogether. They were beautiful, sure, but swimming in open water with marine life of any type seemed dangerous to her.

"So, you're working more than usual?"

He climbed down the ladder, onto the platform that hovered inches above the water.

Slowly, she followed.

"Yeah. Ever since, you know. We're one short."

"Since the incident."

He slipped into the water, and she put on her flippers and followed.

She tried to focus on what he was saying. Treading water in the dark lagoon was proving enough of a workout, and her breathing was starting to get short.

"The other trainer, Baz, he quit straight after."

"Right. So now you're down two."

"Yeah. Not that it matters. The place will be shut down anyway, right?"

Jil looked at him. "Why do you say that?"

"Well, the financial losses, obviously. Isn't that what you're here to figure out?"

Jil kicked herself. "Sort of," she answered, deciding honesty might be the best route to go. "I'm more interested in finding out the truth of what really happened."

He squinted at the sun. "Right. Okay. So, let's say I knew something."

"Okay. Not about dolphins?"

He handed her a buoy and she grabbed it. The flotation device kept her bobbing at the surface and she let out a long breath.

"Thanks. I thought I was a pretty good swimmer."

"Flippers can take some getting used to."

"Aren't they supposed to help?"

"Yeah, but at first they can sort of drag you down too. Just go a bit more horizontal and you'll level out."

Jil leaned back into the water until she found her equilibrium. "If you did have something to say, I'd be happy to hear it."

"This is the only place where nobody could be listening."

"You have something to tell me?"

"You don't look much like an accountant."

"Yeah? What does an accountant look like?"

"Well, this one looks like a PI."

Jil stared at him. She'd never been made so easily before.

"If you are a PI, I'm glad."

"Why would you be glad?"

"Because the gendarme here suck. They're not looking into this shit at all. There's no way Tasha would have been stupid enough to get anywhere near Tsunami when she was alone. She knew her story. She was careful. And smart. This was her dream job. And if Tsunami had killed her, she would have eaten her, not carried her around for a ride on her back."

"What do you think happened?"

"I dunno, man. I just know the gendarme have been wanting this place closed for years. No idea why. They just came in, strung up their yellow tape over everything, and started posting up notices. Doesn't seem to matter to them that someone was trying to kill the whale."

Jil frowned. "How? Who told you this?"

"Tasha."

"What did she say, exactly?"

"She didn't know for sure. Only that the fish he was eating smelled strange. She thought it had gone off, so she tossed it out."

"Where?"

"Into the garbage bin at the back of the sea aquarium. She got Tsunami new food, but…"

A dolphin chattered across the lagoon, and Jil braced herself.

"Just relax. They haven't drowned anyone in years."

She gave him the slit eye and he smiled.

"When she left for the day, she noticed the dead seagulls near the bin."

"How many?"

"I don't think she stopped to count them. She said she didn't even clue in right away—that they might have eaten the fish."

"But birds eat rotten fish all the time."

"That's what she realized. Later. When we were back in residence. She wanted to come back to check it out, but we were all going out for the night and so she waited till morning."

"And?" Jil's legs were beginning to feel like overcooked spaghetti.

"When she got here, they were gone. The bin was empty."

"Is it possible that someone just cleaned up the dead fish so they wouldn't stink up the park?"

"Yeah, it's definitely possible. It's just weird, that's all. Weird enough that Tasha would say something. There's a lot of people's jobs on the line here. Animals' lives at stake. If you were a PI, I'd be glad someone was looking into the truth. That's all."

Jil nodded. "Well, as far as I know, I woke up an accountant and I'll go to sleep an accountant. But if I were a PI, I'd be glad you shared that with me."

Max smiled and put his whistle in his teeth. He let out a quick blast and a dolphin popped up next to Jil.

She gasped.

"Hold out your hand," Max said.

Jil extended her arm just in time, and the smooth gray skin touched her fingertips as the dolphin glided by, then ducked out of sight.

"They're denser than I thought."

"Everyone says that. Wait till you ride one."

"Ride one? I'm not riding one."

The dolphin bumped her with her nose and she laughed.

"Hey!"

Max grabbed onto the dolphin's dorsal fin with two hands, holding himself slightly up and over the animal's broad back. And with a powerful downstroke of her tail, Koko had him halfway across the tank. They sped in a circle, reminding Jil of a circus performer standing on a horse's bare back.

"That was awesome."

Max reached into the bucket and gave Koko a fish. She chittered and gulped it down.

"God, they're smart, aren't they?" Jil said.

"They are. Smart enough to teach you how to ride one." And before she could object, Max had guided her hands onto the dolphin's dorsal fin. "Hang on tight."

She felt the instinctive reflex of the dolphin's muscles under her and held on for dear life as she was skimmed around the tank, water spurting over her head and body. She counted three, four seconds before she fell off. Coughing and sputtering, she surfaced.

"Wow."

"Not bad for your first ride."

Max gave her a thumbs-up from across the lagoon.

Something bumped her from underneath and she turned around to see Koko's black eyes staring at her. She didn't know if dolphins could laugh, but it sure looked like it.

"Thanks for the ride," Jil said.

Koko body-rubbed her, reminding her unexpectedly of Zeus, asking for a pet.

She rubbed the dolphin's head and back.

"Heads up!"

She turned just in time to see Max toss her a fish to give to Koko, but the dolphin caught it herself and dove down.

"That was amazing," Jil said after she'd swum back to the dock. "Exhausting, but amazing."

"You're not a bad swimmer," Max said.

"Not bad, per se, but definitely not stellar."

The fish in the bucket had reminded her...

"Hey, one more question."

"Sure."

"Besides you, did Tasha tell anyone about the fish?"

Max thought for a sec.

"Yeah, actually, I think she did."

"Who?"

He hauled himself out of the water, then turned to help Jil out as well.

"Ramone."

CHAPTER FOURTEEN

This physical aspect to decision making was something Jess still struggled to understand. Forgot about, actually, until it happened to her. How she'd be wrestling with a decision, wracked with anxiety, guilt, confusion. How she'd make pro and con lists. Pray, occasionally—when she still felt like she could do that.

And how, one day, she'd just wake up and the decision would have been made for her, almost as if her dreams had sorted out the facts and now her body could act. She'd pick up the phone or get in the car. Make the appointment or cancel the event. Say yes or say no.

Her body would decide.

And this morning, as her eyes opened and the first light of the new day washed over her, she had decided.

She was going to quit her job. Resign.

As the coffee filtered down into the carafe, she emailed the superintendent and asked him to meet her at nine a.m.

He would be busy, but he would make time for her, she knew it. Within minutes, he'd responded. *Meet you at St. Mag's. Already there for the morning.*

She tried to call Jil, but it went straight to voice mail. Instead, she texted.

You were right. Meeting with the Spr this morning. Call you when it's done.

She poured a cup of coffee and stood looking out the window while she drank it.

This house would have to go on the market. She would have to move. She could do that, now that he was dying.

Dying.

Hadn't he been dying for years?

She sat on the window seat and watched the kids getting on the school bus. She smiled sadly. Their little backpacks, their little hats.

Maybe it was just that she missed teaching elementary school. The kids had been so cute with their earnest expressions and their forthright renditions of their home lives. But something deeper clawed at her when she looked at those little ones. Motherhood. A chance she'd never taken, and now, could never endure.

"Jessie, how do we know if we don't try? Who knows what kind of parents we'd be?"

"I'm not even thirty yet. Don't you want to wait?"

"Thirty. Geez," he teased her. "I thought with your ambitious nature, you'd want to pop out two or three before that."

She turned away from him and he rubbed a hand on her shoulder, kissed her neck like he was sorry for bringing it up. She didn't shrink away from him, but she also didn't turn around. Just let her arm drape over the side of the bed, keeping the same distance from him.

How could they possibly think of being parents right now? Someday, maybe. Probably. But now? They'd talked about it. Agreed in their marriage preparation courses. They'd made a plan, and that had involved kids. She knew that. She remembered talking about it with Mitch and Father McGillivray. And she remembered, quite clearly, that she'd been telling the truth when she said she wanted kids.

But if she wanted it someday, shouldn't she at least be able to imagine it now? She couldn't. What it would feel like to have her stomach expanding, a tiny person inside her, kicking to get out? Mitch playing the guitar or the clarinet every night after dinner.

How was it that some parts made sense? That a cooing baby could produce a longing so strong she had to look away from the chubby cheeks, the bright, perfect eyes. That she could happily wander through the baby boutiques, picking out a crib, admiring quilts and stuffed animals. Fingering onesies and bibs...little dresses. She could imagine holding a baby, smelling him, rocking her to sleep and singing lullabies as she nursed.

She knew how babies were made. She knew she needed him to produce one inside her. And Mitch would be a good father. He'd be there for baseball games or clarinet practice or whatever their child was into.

But whenever he moved to touch her, she turned away. Not always. And not bluntly. But consistently.

She went to Confession.

"I want a baby but I don't want sex, Father."

"Usually it's the other way around, my daughter. Remember your wifely duties. Perhaps you are just tired."

Three Hail Marys and a trip to the lingerie store.

And just before Christmas, she found out she was expecting.

Five weeks in and she wrapped a little ornament in a box to put under the tree.

Maybe it was premonition that had stopped her. Changed her mind. Maybe she'd known, somewhere in the recesses of her subconscious, that it wasn't meant for her.

Perhaps it was a blessing, in the end, not having to raise an infant by herself. But maybe, if they'd had the baby, he wouldn't have gone on that trip. Maybe he would have stayed home to look after the baby. Maybe he wouldn't have been driving angry. And frustrated.

There were so many possibilities.

That night, the night before they would cross the threshold to the second trimester—the time when they could officially tell everyone they'd unofficially told—she'd felt a cramping in her pelvic floor. A light, niggling feeling around the perimeter.

She stretched. Took a bath. Looked it up in the pregnancy book that sat dog-eared on her nightstand. Mild cramping toward the second trimester might indicate that baby was growing.

Fine.

But she didn't feel fine. She felt heavy and tired. Anxious. She checked her underwear in the bathroom. No spotting. Just that dull, heavy feeling.

"Go to bed, Jessie. You're tired. Pregnancy has aches and pains, remember?"

She did remember little bands of women at baby showers, birthday parties—talking ad nauseam about the nausea and the vomiting, the swollen ankles and tender breasts. She'd absorbed it, as women absorb the story of motherhood from other women: lightly, letting their experiences wash over her and sketch the outlines for what she should expect.

At the time, she didn't understand how different it would feel when it was her turn. How everything she'd heard would somehow make a different kind of sense. How she'd feel betrayed, all the same, that nobody had explained to her exactly what would happen. Exactly how it would feel.

How scared she'd be.

"C'mon. Lie down." Mitch wrapped her up and kissed her forehead.

She went to bed, hoping in the morning the cramping would be gone and everything would be okay. But by two a.m., she knew it wouldn't be.

"Mitch." She hit him lightly in the arm and he woke up.

He turned over and saw her. Saw the blood on her nightgown. On the sheets.

"God, Jessie. Oh shit. What do I do?" He sprang out of bed, wearing only his boxers. As she sat, paralyzed, he groped for

his jeans. Flipped on the overhead light. In the half-shadows, it hadn't looked that bad, but in the full halogens, their bed looked like a crime scene.

Jess looked down to the warm pooling sensation between her legs. She'd never seen so much blood.

Mitch grabbed the phone. Dialed and hung up. Dialed and hung up.

"Nine-one-one," she prompted him weakly. Her belly clenched. The pain was dull and fierce at once. A vice in her lower back. A stabbing in her belly. And the warm gush of blood.

She tried to move toward the bathroom. Save the bed. But as soon as she stood up, the edges of her vision began to darken.

"Don't move, Jessie."

He dialed a third time.

"She looks so pale," she heard him say. "I think she's passing out. Oh fuck."

She felt his arm around her, warm, strong as she slipped under. Toward the floor. Face against the carpet.

In the distance, sirens.

And now, as she sat in the kitchen watching the kids get on the bus, sirens. The sound pulled her away from the memory. An ambulance coming down the street.

It turned off. Down the main road, heading to the hospital. Jess made the sign of the cross and said a quick prayer for whomever it carried, then rinsed her coffee mug in the sink and put it in the dishwasher.

It was a brand-new appliance; she'd replaced it last fall. She'd heard that new appliances made a house easier to sell.

She'd take Jil's advice and call the Realtor, too.

She'd tell the Realtor about Mitch. He'd see a grieving soon-to-be-widow. That would quell the gossip as well. Gossip that only a year ago she wouldn't have been able to tolerate and now couldn't care less about.

Let them talk. Yes, she would be a widow. A disabled widow. A disabled lesbian widow.

So fucking what?

Mitch was dying and there would be a Mass. She'd have to see everyone, but somehow that thought was vaguely comforting. Like a battle she could prepare for—get it all done at once. Shake hands with everyone. Greet them with smiles, even if she had to be pushed in a fucking wheelchair up the aisle because she couldn't make it from the door to the altar.

There was a time when the thought of anyone seeing her stumble would have gored her, but being the pillar of strength had exacted too great a toll and she just felt exhausted. She didn't care. She almost welcomed the pitying glances because at least if they pitied her they wouldn't blame her.

All her teachers. All her students. Her community. They would all think the reason she resigned was because her husband had died and her body had given up on her. It was almost too convenient to be allowed. A blessing, a mercy she didn't deserve.

Mitch—equal parts beard and shield, and even in death, protecting her.

In no way did she deserve that from him, or from God.

CHAPTER FIFTEEN

Jil bought an ice cream and walked down to the edge of the harbor. She and Jess had been missing each other all morning and had finally just given up and texted, with half-hour gaps between replies. With luck, they'd be able to connect tonight. It sounded like Jess was having a doozy of a day.

Jil had decided to take a taxi into town and see if she could find out anything about Baz, Tasha's missing boyfriend.

"Heard he works at the wharf now," Rebecca had said. "Catching fish or something. Can't imagine him doing it, with what he'd get paid, but whatever he wants now, I suppose."

Jil's phone buzzed again. Another missed call from Jess. What the hell? It hadn't even rung. She tried dialing back, but it went straight to voice mail.

"On or off!"

She looked up just as the edge of the swing bridge began to move away from the side of the canal. Jil hopped up on the bridge as the warning siren sounded. People ran off either side and jumped onto the docks as the bridge began to detach from the sides. Soon it was swinging into a horizontal position, two motors pushing it to one side of the canal.

"Thought you were gonna go headfirst into the water, staring at that phone."

A stocky man grinned at her from his post inside the booth that controlled the bridge. She smiled back ruefully, and his dark chocolate face split into a wreath of smiles that showed off his missing front tooth.

"Tourists. Too busy taking pictures to notice the ground is moving."

She grabbed a railing as the bridge swung out into the middle of the harbor. At the entrance of the canal, huge cargo vessels cruised in.

"Okay, okay," the man muttered to a small boat speeding too close to the moving bridge. "Wait a minute. We're getting out of the way. Damn harbor masters."

"How long does the bridge stay closed for?"

"An hour. Two hours. Depends on how much is coming in. Ferries are starting, though."

Jil watched as small ferry boats began to jet across the canal in either direction. They darted in front and behind the slow-moving cargo boats, taking two or three trips in between each.

In the distance, she spotted a cruise ship.

"Two big cruise ships today. Four cargo vessels. It's busy, busy this time of year."

"What's coming in?"

"Oh, everything. Everything the island needs to survive. Food, clothing, building supplies. Tourists." He gave a laugh. "You name it, it comes in through this port."

"Anything come in that's not supposed to?"

He guffawed. "See those guys over there?"

Jil followed his finger point. "Yeah."

"That's their job. All day, every day. Harbor masters. Jump from one ship to another—the big ones, the small ones—looking for anything and everything. Cocaine, heroin, marijuana, prescription drugs, firearms. You name it, people try to smuggle it."

"Why here?"

He shrugged again. "Convenient gateway, I guess. Out in the middle of nowhere. Huge ships, lots of places to hide things. Lots of visitors traveling in and out every day."

Jil nodded.

"What's the biggest bust you've ever heard of?"

He thought. "This year? A case full of protein powder containers. You can guess it didn't contain protein powder."

"Wow."

"Yep. Once heard of a pallet of rifles arriving in a DIY house kit. I could tell you some stories."

"I'll bet."

Another boat sped by, narrowly missing the bridge.

"You'll wanna slow down, man," he muttered. "Always in a rush, these ones. In a right mood about something."

"What is it?"

He shrugged. "Don't like to repeat gossip, but I hear…I hear, there's someone moving some hot powder in and out. Not the usual suspects. And the captain of the gendarme is something pissed about it."

The side of the bridge glided smoothly along the side of the canal, and Jil spotted a ladder that led up to the top.

"This is me," she said.

The guy grinned. "Going shopping?"

"Why not? Can you tell me where I might find the fish market?"

"Turn left when you get up there, heading toward the wharf. You'll smell the ocean. That's the fish."

"Thanks."

Finishing her ice cream, which was melting fast in the Caribbean sun, Jil sauntered down to the wharf. Boats were anchored in the shallow water, offloading their catch onto the docks. Tables filled with ice lined the wharf, and Jil walked up and down, marveling at all the different species.

"Red snapper, miss?"

"No, thank you." She kept moving, until she spotted a tall young guy with freckles and blue hair.

Casually, she approached his booth. How many teenagers working the wharf would match this description?

"Hey. Any recommendations for dinner tonight?" she said to him.

He looked up. Barely. "How many people?"

"Just me."

He grabbed a lobster. Only it wasn't like any lobster Jil had ever seen. "Can't beat it."

He smiled, but it was a surface greeting. Not reaching his eyes by any stretch.

"It's not what you'll be expecting from a lobster. It tastes different from the North American kind, but it's an experience you've got to try."

"Sure. Thanks. You know a lot about fish?"

"Fish, mammals, any sea life really."

"Ever ridden a dolphin?"

He cracked a smile. "Once or twice. During my old job."

She paid him for the lobster. "During your work at the aquarium?"

He flinched. "You're kind of curious, aren't you?"

"I understand it was your girlfriend who was killed at the sea aquarium."

He looked down. "Yeah, that's right."

She smiled. "Is there somewhere we can go to talk?"

"What are you, the police?"

She shook her head. "No. But I hear the police aren't exactly on the ball with this investigation."

Was it her imagination, or had he blushed just then? She decided to cut the crap.

"I'm a PI. I've been hired to look into this case. I would think you'd be happy to know someone's examining it more closely."

"Look, I'm busy right now. I loved my job and I loved my girlfriend, but I want to put it behind me now. The police have shut the case and I need to get on with my life. Okay?"

"You aren't curious to know what really happened?"

"I know what really happened. Tasha went somewhere she wasn't supposed to and she paid the price. She's gone and that's it. I have nothing more to say."

She decided to try a different tack. "I hear you were supposed to be on a date the night she was killed."

His Adam's apple bobbed and she tried to catch his eye, but he wouldn't look at her.

"Yeah, that's right. She told me to pick her up at the aquarium. Said she had something to take care of after hours—that she would explain when I picked her up."

"Did it have something to do with the poisoned fish she found?"

Baz looked up. "How do you know about that?"

She didn't answer.

"I don't know. She didn't say. I told her maybe it wasn't a good idea to be sneaking around after hours."

"Why?" Jil interrupted.

"Well, just, you know…" Baz stammered.

"No, I don't know. If I wanted to go into my work place after hours, I wouldn't expect to come to any harm, so why did you warn your girlfriend about doing that?"

He blushed red. "It's just, you know. There are animals there. It's a different scene at night when the lights are off and the shows aren't on. When it's just you and an orca, or you and a pod of dolphins. They're wild animals, miss. You know?"

Jil nodded. She'd seen what a pissed-off whale could do. "Yeah."

"Anyway," Baz turned to sling some more fish onto the cutting board, "I'm busy now, okay? I've got to get back to work. My mother's already pissed off enough that I quit the aquarium.

Can't afford to get fired from this job too. She'd have the entire gendarme after me."

"Why?" Jil asked.

Baz smiled weakly. "Captain's privilege."

Jil stared at him. Now she saw the resemblance. Baz's hair was longer than his mother's, but he had her build: petite and fluid, with nut brown skin and a straight nose.

"Your mother's the captain of the gendarme?"

He rolled his eyes. "Try getting into any trouble at all as a kid."

She smiled tightly. "Sure. I get it. But if there's ever anything you want to discuss, feel free to give me a call." She handed over her business card and left with her lobster.

Damn.

When she looked up, she saw a flash of blue hair heading toward the taxi stand. She frowned. Quickly, she turned around and followed him, keeping three or four people between them. Maybe he was chatting to a friend.

Baz leaned into the window of a cab, and Jil ducked behind a restaurant sign, pretending to scroll through her phone as she watched. Unpleasant looking guy. Older, rough. They didn't smile at all. Not friends then.

Baz handed over something and the guy reached into his pocket and gave Baz a sack, almost like a pencil case.

Baz shoved it in his pocket and walked away.

Jil put her phone into her pocket, ninety percent sure she'd just witnessed an illegal transaction.

CHAPTER SIXTEEN

Jess drove around the side of the school to the teachers' parking lot, observing that her spot was filled with a black Lexus. Instead, she took a spot in the main lot.

Not the accessible slot. She couldn't stand that at her own school.

The door was heavy, almost too heavy, and the familiar scent of cafeteria food, sweat, and wood shavings hit her the second she opened the door. It hurt her stomach physically, being in that building.

She should have met him at the school board office. Why did it have to be here?

She walked into the atrium.

"Hat," she said automatically.

A student took off his baseball cap and stuffed it in his backpack.

"Hi, Miss. Are you back?"

She looked at the two senior girls. They wore gym suits. One carried a basketball. She wondered if the team was on track for championships.

"No," she replied. She smiled but didn't fill in the blanks. Not yet. Soon. Never, actually.

I'm meeting with the superintendent right now to resign.

Resign.

The meeting lasted five minutes.

"My husband is dying. My illness is getting worse. This job is just too stressful."

Words that had sat in her mind like shards of glass, piercing her thoughts, her heart—words she never thought she'd have to say—she used to cut the cord that had been strangling her for the past year.

She handed in her notice. She walked away.

Then she got in her car and drove to the hospital.

The day was interminable. And driving home that night, alone, she wished more than anything that Jil were waiting for her.

Hours later, Jess's tablet finally rang.

She hit *Accept* and Jil's face swam into view.

"How are you?" Jil asked immediately.

Jess shrugged. "Pretty good for a liar."

"It's not exactly a lie, Jess." Jil's voice made Jess want to crawl through the screen and into her arms. "You are leaving for health reasons. Emotionally, you're exhausted. Physically, you're a train wreck. What exactly did you expect to be able to sustain before caving? And when would you let yourself? Never."

Jess pulled the blanket more tightly around her shoulders and picked up her glass of Carnivor. The wine warmed her insides and helped dull the ache in her joints.

"Well, now," she returned. "Now I don't have a choice."

"No, you don't. Your body is saying enough and your heart needs a rest. So rest."

"I am resting."

She looked past Jil's face at the view from her balcony, the green margarita in her hand and the sun going down over the ocean. A million miles away.

"I mean the internal dialogue."

"That, I can't seem to turn off."

Jil exhaled and something clinked, like ice in a glass. "What is it? Tell me the problem."

"I feel like an imposter. Like I'm getting sympathy I don't deserve."

"Because you fell in love with a woman?"

Jess felt tears welling up in her eyes, hot and thick in her throat. "Twice," she whispered.

"More the second time, though, right?" Jil said. Something about the way she said it made Jess pause. Like she didn't quite believe it.

"Yeah," she said seriously. "A lot more the second time."

"You deserve to be loved, Jess. And to have someone make love to you the way I want to make love to you right now."

Jess closed her eyes as the memory of Jil's hands on her body made her heart race. "I do like that," she said.

"I know."

"It might even be worth eternal damnation."

Jil whispered, "I don't believe in that."

"I know."

"There's enough hell on earth, Jess. Nobody's waiting to punish us for loving each other and doing our best in this life."

Jess let the tears fall down her face. Tonight everything was just too heavy, and she wanted to sink into a bath in the dark and let it all wash over her head.

"Remember the lavender salts. It'll help you sleep," Jil said.

She laughed softly at the way Jil could read her mind sometimes. "Good night. I love you," she said.

"Same here, babe. See you soon."

Jess sat on the side of the tub, waiting for it to fill, but the memories kept coming, hot and fast, like tears she'd rather not shed. The water filled, she added lavender and watched the mini bomb break apart, pieces floating to the surface before dissolving.

Her mind was on a backward track. On a loop replaying her life with Mitch in the beginning.

Had she ever loved him like she loved Jil?

She was young. Twenty-six, maybe. Not even? She'd met him at a cottage in Muskoka during a teacher training outdoor ed seminar. More like a weeklong cottage party.

Hotdog and marshmallow roasts. Campfire songs.

Mitch played the guitar, she sang—loud, ridiculous camp songs left over from her childhood at sleepaway camps. Then, as the night wore on, and the fire went from a roaring blaze to a dull glow of hot embers, he handed her the guitar and she played something soft—she couldn't remember what.

She'd never gotten used to playing a string instrument that way, slung across her knees, strumming with her fingers instead of a bow, but she made do. He watched her pick out chords, translating them from the vertical position of a cello to the horizontal position the guitar needed.

They'd stayed up late, trading stories, histories. He was a fascinating person, lively and smart. She'd fallen in love with him so quickly.

Thought she'd fallen in love with him.

And now she was forced to ask herself—had she ever been in love with him?

The water reached the bottom of the silver circle and she shut it off. She slipped into the hot liquid embrace, feeling her muscles unclench almost immediately. But her mind didn't. It wouldn't stop churning.

A year ago, she would have said yes. Yes, of course she'd loved him.

But the way Jil looked at her—dark eyes probing every inch of her face, her soul. The way they slipped into conversation, barely a thread dropped, speaking with nothing more than a gesture, a look. The deep understanding they had—like they would always be on the other's side, no questions asked. The way they checked in, listened, acted without being asked—she'd never felt that with Mitch.

The way Jil touched her, barely touched her, and she came with such fierceness, so completely—her whole body trembling and releasing. Never, with Mitch, had she felt like that, collapsed like that. Fallen asleep, entwined, never wanting to be let go.

Had she?

She couldn't remember.

But that didn't mean she didn't love him, did it?

It had just been different, right?

The water didn't answer, but she knew the answer. And she held her breath and slipped under the surface, trying to drown out the thoughts she'd never before let herself think.

CHAPTER SEVENTEEN

I'd like your permission to do a stakeout," Jil said.
Rebecca made a face. "A stakeout? Here?"
She nodded.
"What for? What have you found out?"
Rebecca closed the door to her office and Jil took a seat.
"A few interesting things. But I'd rather not say yet until I know anything for certain. In my experience, the less everyone knows, the better. And by everyone, I mean anyone but me."
Rebecca switched on the coffeemaker and popped a pack into the machine.
"You want a coffee?"
"No thanks. I've rejected single-use plastic."
Rebecca looked at her. "I have instant. Would you like that?"
"I'll have iced tea if you have that."
Rebecca smiled. "We always have that." She opened the fridge and leaned down to grab the jug. Then she leapt back, screaming.
"What?" Jil jumped up.
Rebecca backed away from the fridge.
"It's…it's…"
Jil looked down. "An eyeball."
"Look in the bottom shelf. God, oh gross."
Jil pulled out a Tupperware container that contained eyeballs floating in a gelatinous substance. She almost lost her lunch.
"Who the hell would put that in there?"

"I don't know, but that's disgusting. Jesus."

Jil peered closer. "They're too small to be human. Human eyeballs are actually really big, once they're dislodged from the skull."

Rebecca stared at her. "Thank you very much, Doctor. Can you please get the hell rid of that while I find out what sicko has put that in the staff food fridge?"

She picked up her radio and stormed out while Jil shrugged and helped herself to some iced tea.

A few moments later, the doorknob turned and Leonard came in, munching a hot dog.

"Hey. How's it going?"

Jil smiled. "Fine. Just waiting on Rebecca."

"You might be waiting a while. She's all up in arms. Eyeballs or something?"

"See for yourself," Jil said.

Leonard opened the fridge door and winced. "That's gross. They're fish eyes." He shut the door and pitched the rest of his hotdog in the garbage.

"Hey, I'm heading out to see how the repairs are going on the shipwreck observatory. You want to come along? See what the repair costs actually look like in real time?"

Jil shrugged. "Sure." She had nothing else to do while Rebecca chased down the fish-eye suspect.

"This shipwreck was hauled from the shore through the lagoon to the back of the sea aquarium about ten years ago. It's been used as a tourist feature. Who doesn't love a half-sunk ship where you can go below deck? It's got an oversized window that we installed especially for that purpose. Unfortunately, it might be more to repair than it's worth."

"That's too bad."

"It is. It's my favorite underwater observatory."

Leonard swung himself into the hole and began descending the ladder into the half-sunk boat. Once again, Jil marveled at his agility with his prosthetic device. It seemed like a natural extension of his leg. No limp, no hesitation.

"This is as close as I get to predators in the sea," he quipped. "Triple-paned glass, which is a good thing because water pressure is a pretty amazing thing."

Jil followed him down.

"So how long have you been a tax accountant?"

Jil hesitated, her mind racing for a way to avoid being in a numbers conversation with the numbers guy. "It's a second career for me," she hedged. "Not glamorous, but it pays the bills."

"I could never do it myself," Leonard said. "Too much baggage."

Jil laughed. "I know what you mean. Say the word 'taxes' and everybody runs for the hills. Hey, tell me what I'm seeing here."

Anything to change the subject before he asked her to recite the tax code or something. She looked out into the murky water as a shadow passed.

"This is our friend Michelangelo."

Jil took a step back as a giant fish glided out of the darkness and past the porthole.

"Holy shit."

"No kidding. I wouldn't want to run into him underwater. That's a four-hundred-pound grouper right there."

"Do they eat people?"

Leonard grinned. "If provoked."

"Wow."

"Also down here are nurse sharks and stingrays. We're about twenty feet down at the lowest point. Not deep enough to pop your eardrums, but far enough that you wouldn't love most of what you're sharing the water with."

Vibrations from the aft section of the boat made her turn around.

"There's a crew back there reinforcing the hull. It's been leaking," Leonard said. "Actually, we'd probably better head up.

I wouldn't want to be down here if it sprung a leak. The thing's so old it'd probably fill in ten seconds and sink the rest of the way.

Jil followed back up the ladder, and they saw Rebecca striding down to the observation ship.

"That's my cue," Leonard said and gave Jil a small salute as he hightailed it in the opposite direction.

"Nobody's copping to it," said Rebecca as she caught up to Jil.

"Do you blame them? You're a bit fierce right now."

Rebecca gave her a withering look. "I think I've earned my stripes."

"Possibly, but in my experience, listening works better than bludgeoning."

Rebecca took a deep breath. "Maybe. Anyway, I wanted to tell you that you're fine to hold your little stakeout if you still want to."

Jil grinned. "Yes. I do. Thanks."

"I'll leave you my pass card when I go home tonight so you can move about. I don't know what you expect to find, but you can brief me in the morning. I'm going home right at closing tonight. I have a headache and a thousand emails to answer."

At five minutes to five, Jil ducked into the locker room and made her way over to the storage cage that held the equipment. A wall of lifejackets along one side dripped a steady stream on to the floor. Floatation devices of all sorts lay stacked on a floor-to-ceiling plastic shelf, and the corner was stacked with mats. The floor was also padded, she noticed—hard rubber mats that would make it more difficult to hear people coming in and out.

She didn't know what she expected to find either, but she'd noticed over her career that the facility of the daytime and the facility of nighttime were often two completely different animals.

Anyone who needed time to sabotage, steal, cover something up, or do anything else illegal or immoral would need the cover of darkness and some privacy to do it.

With the way things were going, it seemed obvious that someone on the inside of this place was intent on making things miserable for everyone else. And she had another motive for wanting to stay tonight. She wanted to eliminate Rebecca as a suspect. If she was at home, safely, and things were still going down, then Jil would know Rebecca had nothing to do with sabotaging her own sea aquarium. Something she'd seen more than once.

And usually for financial reasons.

Jil made a dry pallet for herself in the corner, inside the cage, and made sure the equipment obscured any view of her. Most of the staff had already left for the night. Now to wait for closing.

By the time she got settled in, her watch read 5:17. Only a quarter of an hour left.

"C'mon, you know we just have to keep it secret a little longer."

Footsteps stopped at the door, then changed to swishing as they came onto the padded locker room floor. Two people, by the sound of it.

"I know. I'm just weirded out by it now."

Their voices were too low to recognize—both male, but that was as much as she could tell. She tried to peek around the stack of equipment, but she'd done a pretty good job making herself invisible. She hadn't imagined she'd want to look *out*.

"It's not like she didn't know, right?"

"No. She knew. She didn't like it, but…"

"So there you go."

"It's just. You know, risky being back here."

Back here?

Jil craned her neck but still couldn't see. Was that Baz's voice she recognized? She listened harder, but they were whispering.

"Yeah. But where else am I going to see you?"

One of them muttered something she couldn't hear.

"…want to make sure it's a for-sure thing with you, you know?"

"I'll try to convince you."

"Here?"

A low chuckle and the unmistakable sound of kissing, then soft groaning.

Jil ducked lower in the cage. Well, this was awkward. She looked at her watch: 5:29. Unlikely anyone would walk in and interrupt them.

The breathing grew harsher, louder, and one of them started moaning over and over again. Then the other one started. She bit her lip to keep from giggling, remembering her own near-encounter with Jess at the spa.

She slid down as far as she could go, waiting for them to be finished. Were they seriously having sex on top of an old floating dock covered in soggy mats? She rolled her eyes.

At last, with one final groan, they stopped.

"C'mon. Let's get the place cleaned so we can get out of here. Grab some dinner or something."

"Yeah. Sounds good."

"When do you start at the new place?"

"Monday."

"Good. Make sure you keep your head down and your nose clean. Make them trust you."

"What are you, my daddy?"

A laugh. "Would you like that?"

She kept her eye on the door to see if she could spot who left, but the angle was wrong. She'd have to stand up and risk knocking something over. The first one left the room, and she slowly, slowly inched her way up.

A flash of blue hair.

It was him.

Baz. Tasha's boyfriend.

Having sex with another guy.

Well, that was interesting.

When the door finally closed, she breathed a huge but silent sigh of relief and flexed her shoulders, stretching out the cramped muscles she hadn't dared to move.

She went over the roster of staff in her mind, trying to figure out who the other guy might have been but came up empty. It could be any of the guys who worked there.

She checked her email while munching on a granola bar, waiting for silence to fall. That was interesting: the financials had come back on Ramone, and apparently, he owed a lot of money. More than he would make working here… Her stomach dropped. Damn. She really didn't want to like him for this.

She clicked off her phone.

According to her intel, the cleaning and lockup should take only an hour. With those two she'd just witnessed, she wouldn't be surprised if it took ten minutes.

At seven o'clock, she stood up, stretched again, and crept out of the cage.

Nothing.

She opened the door to the storage room, peeked out into the hall, then made her way slowly along the hallway to the stairs.

Still nothing.

At the door to the upper floor where the front entrance was, she stopped and looked out the window. A light shone down the hallway near Rebecca's offices.

And a person walked across.

Who was that?

She checked her watch.

Nobody should be here at this hour. She pressed on the bar to open the door slowly, slowly, so it didn't squeak, and let it close behind her. Keeping to the shadows, she crept through the atrium by the front admissions desk and down the hall toward the indoor aquariums.

A sliver of light shone from under a door in one of the rear workrooms. And a puddle had formed on the concrete floor, leaking out from under the door.

She frowned. That was the space where the staff cut fish, got together the food for the animals, and went through practice drills. It was also where they brought animals that needed medical attention. It held observation tanks and holding enclosures. A giant bed for sharks with mechanisms to stream water over them so they could breathe without being submerged. She'd seen it all on her first day, but this hadn't been where she'd expected to catch a killer…

Avoiding the puddle, she leaned closer to the door.

A voice, loud and jovial, made her stop.

"Good evening and welcome to this edition of *Fish Facts*."

Quietly, she turned the knob to the door and pushed it open.

Ramone turned around, a lobster in his hand. His jaw unhinged.

"What are you doing here?"

He stopped and stared, then quickly shut off the camera that was set up on the table beside him.

Jil folded her arms over her chest.

"Better question—what are *you* doing here?"

His mouth opened and closed for a few seconds, then he put the lobster down on the platform.

Jil looked at the setup on the metal counters. The animals lined up along the platform.

Ramone sighed.

"I'm making a YouTube video, okay?"

"A YouTube video? Why? About what?"

He opened a small underwater cage and tucked the lobster inside.

In another tank, a shark flipped its tail, sending another wave of water cascading over the side. Adding to the puddle.

"Isn't that tank a bit small for him?"

Ramone looked over. "It's only for a few minutes. I wanted a guaranteed close-up shot." He looked at the puddle on the floor. "Another insult to injury. The fridge went out earlier this morning. Then this."

"The fridge?"

"Yeah. Which is why..."

He stopped.

Jil laughed. "Which is why you had to store your fish eyeballs in the staff fridge?"

Ramone sighed. "Don't say anything. I needed them for tonight's episode."

Jil crowed. "Disgusting. Oh my God. What are you doing, anyway?"

"My oldest. She got accepted into a really good school, okay? In the States. And I can't afford it. Not on what I make. I made the deposit by the skin on my teeth."

Ah. That would explain the financials.

"Then I met this guy. A tourist. Told me all about multiple income streams. How I should start a YouTube channel. Get some followers. Make a few extra bucks."

Jil relaxed. "Is it working?"

"Yeah." Ramone's face lit up. "The trouble is, I don't have any animals of my own. So I gotta beg and borrow."

"And Rebecca doesn't know this?"

Ramone's shoulders slumped. "I meant to tell her. I did. But I thought I'd better try it first, you know, see if I could actually do it. Just a trial run. Then I started thinking, what if she said no? What if she charged me to use them? Then everything that happened with Tsunami and all that, she was busy. So I just figured it wasn't over until the fat lady sings. If she shut me down, I'd have to tell my baby girl that I couldn't send her to that fancy college..."

"So you sneak in after hours and exploit the sea aquarium's marine population for your own financial gain?"

Ramone stared at her. "Geez, man—when you say it like that, I sound like a real criminal."

Jil laughed. "I don't think filming YouTube videos is high on the list of felonies."

"You'll keep the cat in the bag, won't you?"

Jil considered for a moment. "There's something I need to know, Ramone."

"Anything."

"Were you here the night Tasha was killed?"

He let out a long breath. "Yes," he said at last. "But I didn't see her, I swear. I was filming, and left around seven thirty. Nobody else was in the building. I didn't mention it, obviously…"

"Because you didn't want to be the last one who saw her alive."

"Exactly. But I swear when I left, there was nobody else here."

Jil sighed. "Okay, I'll tell you what—I'll keep your YouTube channel…in the bag…if you help me with something."

Ramone looked at her as if something had just dawned on him. "What are you doing here anyway? How'd you get in?"

A lifetime of people watching had taught Jil something important, and that was if her gut trusted a person, that person was usually trustworthy.

"I'm trying to figure out what really happened to Tsunami."

Ramone lifted his chin like he wasn't all that surprised to hear it.

"So you were looking around here tonight, seeing if you could find anything…suspicious?"

"Something like that."

"And instead you walked in on my home movies?" He grinned—a broad smile of crooked teeth.

She laughed. It was a relief to know he wasn't her guy. But that meant she had to redouble her efforts to find the truth, because she'd already been made once. Time was working against her.

"What are you, a PI?"

Jil looked at him. "The less you know the better."

"Okay. Fine. I'll keep calling you the tax accountant."

"Good."

They both stopped.

"Did you hear that?" Ramone asked.

Jil headed for the door, Ramone on her heels. They ran down the hall to the front entrance, where the main door stood propped open.

Whoever had been there had gotten out.

She and Ramone exchanged a glance.

"How much do you think they heard?" Ramone asked in a low voice.

"I don't know. But I think we'd better get out of here. You?"

Ramone took her back down the hall to the training room and closed the door.

"Meet me here tomorrow, first thing. I have an idea…"

CHAPTER EIGHTEEN

Mondays had always meant something different to Jess. The top of a new school week. A long list of things to do. Early start, strong coffee, and a rush of adrenaline.

But this Monday started slowly. Time crawled as she sat by Mitch's bedside hour after hour. She found she could barely look at him. As odd and unlikely as it was, she had a fear that he would open his eyes. Stare at her. Reproach her with his look and his words.

How could you?

What were you thinking?

How could you do this to me?

Help me, Jessica.

But of course he just lay there, inert. On his back, on his side, away from her, depending on where the nurses placed him. His breathing had started to get a bit labored. His heart was young and strong, though, Dr. Rabinovitch had reminded her. Not keen to give up the ghost unless it had to.

Which it didn't, apparently. Not yet. So she sat here still, this niggling, irrational fear at the back of her mind.

Shouldn't she be wishing for him to wake up? Wouldn't that be everyone's dream come true? And of course, if she'd been asked, she would have responded that of course that's what she'd want. For him to open his eyes and look at them.

Even if she had to hear the words he deserved to say to her.

Something that Father Gus said yesterday looped around in Jess's mind.

"Maybe it's not only God's forgiveness you need, but also Mitch's."

She hadn't said a word to him except hello since she arrived. She'd just sat there like a mannequin for hours on end, holding his hand or turning on the radio for him, the words swirling around in her head but sticking in her throat.

When will you have another chance?

Speak up. Talk to him. Tell him.

"Hi, Mitch."

She stopped. Her voice sounded hollow and loud in the room. It reminded her of praying out loud in a church and finding out she was the only one speaking.

But slowly, she was able to whisper, and then speak. She'd started at the day of his accident. Told him everything that had happened in the hours after he got hurt. The falling out she'd had with Myra. She'd talked to him like she'd never done when he was awake. Like she'd never been able to do with anyone, actually. Like a running verbal diary that had no pause button. She told him about Lily, the artist she'd met before Jil. When she'd first realized that the problems between her and Mitch might be deeper. Might be her fault.

Fault. Was that the right word?

Nurses came in and turned him. Checked his temperature and came back in with medications. She stood up and stretched.

Then she told him about Jil. How they'd met. How they were now.

How much she loved her.

If he were awake, he would have looked at her. She'd always thought of the anger, the hurt on his face. But now, just for a second, she wondered if he would have understood. If she'd been able to explain it to him in this way. If he would have seen her as his friend and the woman he loved. If he could have forgiven her.

She thought maybe he could.

The door opened. That soft swish and swing, and Myra stood there.

She drew herself up.

"I didn't expect you, Jessica." Steely blue eyes held hers.

Jess sighed. "Good morning, Myra."

"If you wouldn't mind, my prayer group is meeting here in a few minutes."

What would she do if Jess just sat there? Maybe pulled up her chair and pulled out her bible?

"I see. How long do you meet for?"

"An hour. Why? Are you planning to come back? Pull the plug while I'm out of the room?"

Jess sighed. "Myra, it would be better if we could discuss this together in a reasonable way."

Myra snorted. "There's no reasonable way to talk about murdering my son."

"Oh, for God's sake, Myra."

She chuffed in her throat. "And you, taking the Lord's name in vain. A Catholic school principal!"

"Yes, well, I'm not a Catholic school principal anymore."

Myra looked genuinely shocked.

"Yes, that's right," Jess continued. "While you're busy playing holier-than-thou, you're completely blind to what's going on right in front of your face. Aren't you? You're not the only person with feelings, Myra. You're not the only one who loves Mitch and wants to do what's best for him. But you're the only one dragging God into it. As if it's His will that Mitch lie here and suffer longer than necessary when he is going to die anyway."

Myra's eyes filled with tears, and she pressed a hanky to her nose.

"He is dying," Jess said firmly. "And not someday, but someday soon. So if you need to drag it out and pray about it while he lies here getting more and more septic by the hour, it's you that will have to live with it. And you'd better just hope he isn't in pain and can't hear and feel what's going on. Knowing you are prolonging things unnecessarily."

"It's not my choice."

"Yes, it is. It's entirely your choice."

Jess turned around to see a group of women standing in the doorway, jaws hanging.

She muttered excuse-mes and pushed through the crowd, heading for the elevator. Dr. Rabinovitch stood down the hall, talking with another patient, but she avoided him and pressed the button to take her down.

Was it true, what she'd said to Myra?

She was his next of kin. Not challenging her, not insisting on pushing forward was her choice as well. Letting Myra take the responsibility felt justified, but was it fair?

Was it fair?

She could have overridden her years ago too and hadn't.

Was that her fault as well?

Were Mitch's years lying in that bed just as much Jess's responsibility as Myra's?

She rode down blindly. The doors opened on the ground floor and she realized the clanging bells she'd been hearing were the sound of her phone ringing.

She tucked her hair behind her ear as Padraig's face swam into view.

"Jess. Hi. How are you?"

"Hi, yourself." She shook her head. "Sorry. I'm a bit out of it."

"I can't hear you. Is it a bad time? Jil mentioned you were at the hospital a lot."

She moved away from the doors and into the lobby. Light filtered down from the skylight and reminded Jess that it was still daytime outside. Time warped in here.

"No, it's fine. I'm just a bit distracted is all."

"Can't blame you. Sorry to hear about everything that's happened."

"Thanks."

"How are things?"

"Not bad. Okay. Been here a lot since I landed. How are you? How's Ireland?"

"Taking a lot longer than I thought. So, what's the story with Mitch?"

Jess felt her breath restrict. She bit her lip and clenched her teeth as her nose got hot. A sure sign she was going to cry.

"You got time for a cuppa?" Padraig asked.

Jess nodded. "Sure. House is a bit quiet without Jil anyway."

"Well, I'm sure she feels the same way about you."

"I'll call you back when I get to the café?" Jess wondered for a moment why hospital designers always thought putting a cafeteria in the basement was wise. The coffee and cream served up next to the morgue.

"I'll be waiting."

The elevator dinged, and Jess followed the sound of chatter and the smell of tater tots, soon arriving at the busy cafeteria. It reminded her so strongly of the cafeteria at St. Marguerite's that, for a second, she hesitated at the door.

Then a crowd of nurses bustled in behind her and she had to go in.

She stood in line to grab a latte, then found a table way at the back and with only a few stains on it.

As she took her first sip, she called Padraig back.

"So he's not doing well, I gather?" Padraig's eyebrows knitted together like two shaggy caterpillars. Looking at him closer, she realized he must be older than she'd thought. He sipped on a glass of something dark in a crystal glass.

"No. Not looking good. Not looking fast either, though."

He shook his head. "Sorry to hear it. That's the worst of both, isn't it?"

"It definitely makes for some very long days." She avoided looking at him as she stirred cream into her coffee. Her emotions sat so close to the surface, everything felt raw and exposed.

"How are you feeling?" he asked.

She shrugged. "Could do with a vacation."

He smiled. "I tried my best. You can't say I didn't give it a go."

"Well, I wish it had stuck. I'm going a bit stir crazy around here."

"That's what Jil said."

"Have you talked to her a lot?" she asked. She tried not to feel the jealousy that was churning in her gut. She and Jil had been lucky to talk every second day since Jess had come back home.

"Only briefly. I needed her help with something," Padraig said dismissively.

"Wish you'd asked me," Jess said. "I need an escape from my brain."

Padraig's eyes lit up. "Good, I'm glad to hear it. I didn't want to impose on you, but I have a job that needs doing at the hospital, and it seems you're perfect for the job."

"Impose away," Jess said.

"I'd do it myself, but I won't be back in time. If ever."

Jess held her phone closer. "You're not serious. You're not staying?"

He didn't answer. "I've had a few surprises while I've been here. I'll fill you and Jil in another time, but it's been a bit of a trip. Anyway, I need some more time to sort things out. Maybe I'll even do a bit of sightseeing, or God help me, vacationing. I don't want to die of stress before I've seen some of the world."

"Yeah. You can't get back time, can you?"

Mitch probably knew that better than anyone. Thirty-five and his life was over. Forty, and he still hadn't let go of it.

"What's the job anyway?"

He took a sip before answering. "Assignment. Theft."

"What kind of theft?"

"Oh, various things. Nothing big enough for the police to actually take seriously. But it's a nuisance."

"Valuables?"

"Some jewelry, yes. Books. Flowers from patients' rooms. It's odd, but nobody's been able to identify the thief. I don't have time for this case, but the hospital director is an old friend of mine. I said yes before I knew how long I'd be here."

Jess set aside her coffee. It tasted like the burnt bottom of a pot. "So how do I approach it? I don't have much experience as a sleuth."

He looked at her with interest. "That's why you're perfect."

"How's that?"

"Well, you're there for a legitimate reason. Spending a lot of time sitting bedside by the sounds of it."

Jess shrugged. "Can't deny that. And an investigation would certainly help me pass the time doing something besides sniping with Myra. But I don't know anything about how to start."

"You know more about PI work than most people, sleeping with one and all."

Jess cracked a smile. "We do have the most appalling pillow talk. Paperwork and quality of coffee thermoses."

Padraig laughed. "I can imagine."

"What would I have to do, exactly?"

"Well, I can give you a quick crash course. Mainly, sit there. Listen. Have cups of coffee with people in the cafeteria. See if anybody will talk to you about anything that's been missing. Then try to identify a pattern of who has been around when. You know—like trying to figure out which of your students pulled a fire alarm to get out of a math test." He winked.

"Oh. Yeah. I've got plenty of experience with that. If that's all I have to do, I'm perfect for the job."

"That's what I thought. You can start tomorrow. I'll tell them I've got my junior partner on the case."

"So do they have any idea of who's doing it?"

"Well, from the length of time it's been going on, the director figures it has to be an inside job. I've got to agree with him. Two or three years is a long time."

"Any pattern or regularity to it?"

"At least once a week. Often on a Monday, for some reason. The funny thing is that nurses and doctors all rotate shifts. Even the cleaning staff has shift work. So that's what's so peculiar about it. Who's around every week at the same time on the same day? Nobody."

Jess frowned. "Interesting."

Padraig looked at his watch. "I've got to get going, my dear. Someone's arriving soon."

Jess hung up and pitched her coffee in the bin, surprised to notice that she felt better just thinking about having a crime to solve.

CHAPTER NINETEEN

Jil watched the sun come up over the water and sipped her morning coffee. A pelican dove into the shallow surf. Fish were probably as rife along the shallow water as the seaweed that gathered on the shores every night.

She continued to wake up at six—just in time, as it happened, to watch the daily sweeping of the sands. The collection of coconuts. The debris removal that the nightly winds made necessary.

Her phone buzzed with a text from Jess.

I'm up. Are you?

She smiled and texted back. *Caffeine and the ocean. How are things?*

She smiled and hit FaceTime.

"Don't have enough to do without taking on Padraig's caseload and half of mine?"

Jess smiled ruefully. "Anything to keep busy. Anything new to report?"

"Not really. I've been checking all my boxes but I don't have any real leads. I'm hoping something will change soon."

So far, her casual interviews of the staff hadn't yielded very promising results. Most of them had clocked out hours before Tasha's death took place, and she had no proof any of them had come back in after. In fact, there were social media pictures of most of them attending a music gig downtown that started at seven.

Ramone had been at home uploading a YouTube video, which she'd confirmed with the help of some timestamp software, and Leonard had been gone for the weekend. Rebecca Mason had been home alone—something she'd have to come back to.

"I don't know, Jess. All roads seem to lead to the whale killing Tasha, but I just can't seem to make that conclusion and leave."

"Something's bothering you?"

"A few things. One, I'm still waiting on the ME's report. Two, I have requested some info on the insurance, but Leonard's been a bit slow to get it to me. He's drowning in PR."

"I can only imagine," Jess said. "What a nightmare."

She flipped open her laptop and found an email from Rebecca. *Finally got my hands on it. What do you make of this?*

She scanned down the document she'd been waiting to see—the medical examiner's report.

"Hang on. I just got the ME's report."

A head contusion?

She thought for a moment. Could that have happened when she was dragged into the tank? If Tsunami had grabbed her by the ankle, could she have whacked her head on the side?

Did that make sense?

"I've got to go, babe. Can we talk later?"

"Yes, sure. Send me the ME's report and we'll chat later."

Jil smiled and hit forward. Having Jess keep her company on the case was an unexpected pleasure. She'd wait to see what Jess thought of the head injury.

That's what the police had concluded had been the cause of death when they'd shut the case. Her injuries were consistent with a whale attack. End of story.

Jil took her stack of reading out to the deck: "Methods Killer Whales Use to Kill Prey," "Behaviors of Whales in Captivity," and "Psychosis in Intelligent Animals."

She'd watched *Blackfish* over and over again, each time finding more disturbing parallels between the killer orca and

Tsunami. She should have felt like she was wasting her time. Pen any animal in a tank the size of a bathtub and of course it would go nuts. The whale killing the trainer made perfect sense.

Except for the few dissimilarities that bothered her.

First of all, in every instance where a whale had killed or nearly killed a trainer, the whale had been male. Yes, the females were capable of lunging, snapping, and other aggressive tactics, but no female whale had every caused a fatality, as far as she could find.

She scanned back down the document, sorting the medical mumbo jumbo into a neat list of words everyone could understand.

Bleeding head injury.

Teeth marks of whale on arms and legs.

No fatal bite wounds.

Breathed in water. Drowned.

She picked up the phone to call Rebecca.

"So, the official cause of death is drowning?"

Rebecca breathed out a huge sigh. "That's what it says, yeah. And you'll see it in all the newspapers today too."

"They're saying that's evidence the whale killed her, I guess."

"You bet. Here's the *St. Emeline Post*. 'Whale Drowns Young Trainer in Vicious Attack.'"

"Well, I'm no expert, but I've read the report. She had a serious head injury when she went into that tank. And I'm not convinced a whale could've given her that."

Rebecca sighed.

"I'm sorry to have wasted your time, Jil. But I think maybe it's time we pack it in. Official cause of death has been released, and now nobody's going to want to get within ten yards of this whale."

"What are you going to do?"

"What can I do? I can't sell her. I can't keep her. And I can't release her. I'm going to have to euthanize her."

When Jil arrived at the aquarium, she heard the chanting and yelling before she even saw the crowds. Hundreds of protestors had gathered with signs and megaphones, marching up and down the walkway in front of the entrance.

Free Willy.

Captivity = Cruelty

Empty the Tanks

No Death Penalty for Animals

Thinking better of trying to get through the front gates, Jil crossed the footbridge over the lagoon and ducked around the back.

Ramone was waiting for her.

"Heck of a racket, eh?" he said.

"Guess they heard the whale's about to be put down."

Inside the aquarium, Rebecca was, once again, in the observatory. She watched Tsunami slowly moving around and around.

"Leonard's escaping this whole mess. He's signed himself up for every dolphin open water exercise duty there is. Coward." She allowed a tiny smile. "Can't say I blame him. I'd be doing the same."

"I thought he didn't do animals or boats anymore."

"Yeah, well, when your other choice is rabid protestors..."

"Rebecca, I've been doing some reading."

She turned around.

"Of course. And of course you're going to tell me that animals belong in the wild, right? That places like this shouldn't exist."

Jil waited. That had been what she was going to say, actually...

"Well, I can't say I entirely disagree with you. If I were coming in on the same page you're joining in on, I'd be on that side too. Unfortunately, when I bought this place over fifteen years ago, releasing captive animals into the wild wasn't done. It was just assumed they'd die. That they wouldn't be able to survive the transition. That they'd get diseases because their immune systems were suppressed and they'd never been exposed to the toxins or illnesses in the wild."

"But now they've tried it," Jil said.

"Exactly. And they've found that yes, actually, orcas can be released in certain circumstances. That they're brilliant animals. That their families have long lives and long memories."

"But?"

"Do you know that there have only ever been a handful of successful reintegrations of orcas into the wild? The resources that went into making it a success were phenomenal. There's no guarantee it would be successful this time, and then I've just flushed my entire livelihood down the toilet. Not to mention that St. Emeline is a resort island, with this sea aquarium being one major draw. If I close it, do you know how many jobs will be lost? And I'll have to sell the other animals. I can't afford to just release them all. So they'll go from one aquarium to another, and who knows how they'll be treated in the next place? If it were up to me, I like their odds with Ramone as their keeper."

Jil stayed silent. The option of "never having built this aquarium in the first place" didn't exist.

But Rebecca was going on. "We'll lose the therapy aspect. The animal education component. The money for research. There's a lot wrapped up in this place."

"What about just letting Tsunami go?"

Rebecca sighed.

"She'd die and I can't responsibly do that. I have to euthanize her. And either way it'll bankrupt me."

CHAPTER TWENTY

Jess shook some protein powder into her smoothie. She'd had enough of the hospital food and coffee. Her body couldn't handle the grease or the caffeine anymore.

As she made her way to the nurses' station, she watched the activity in and out and around the floor. So many people, so many routes. Unsuspecting patients, families, coming in and out, half asleep, stressed and worried, not even thinking about their handbags or valuables.

This was a thief's paradise.

"Can you tell me where I can store this, please?"

An older nurse got up from the desk, a basket of medication in one hand and a chart in the other.

"Follow me, love."

Jess went with her down the hall and arrived at a little alcove.

"Nurses' fridge is here, but you're welcome to use it if you need to."

"Thanks."

Jess stuck her smoothie in the door.

"It won't get nicked?"

The nurse chuckled. "That, I can't guarantee. Actually, I'd lock up your valuables if I were you. Don't bring them with you."

"Oh, really?" Jess smiled. "Do you think my sweatshirt and flip-flops would count?"

She winked. "You never know what our resident thief will try to take next. Those flip-flops do look comfy."

Jess smiled.

"I lost a pair of sneakers last week. New ones, right out of my locker."

"What?"

"Skechers, size nine."

"Someone stole your shoes?"

"Yes, and I was kicking myself. You'd think I'd know better."

"Yeah, but, wow."

"She's getting more brazen."

"She?"

"The thief."

"How do you know it's a woman?"

The nurse shrugged. "We've guessed. A man in the women's locker room would be noticed."

Jess thought about that. Interesting. "What if he were meant to be there? Like a maintenance person or a repairman?"

"Repairmen around here are once in a blue moon." The nurse pointed up to a light half-hanging from the ceiling. "Four months or more, that one."

Jess made a face. "Nice."

"You should see the state of the sinks. Two out of the five in the locker room are busted."

"Well, that's hygienic."

The nurse's face lit up. "I have an idea."

She set down her chart and grabbed a pen and label from the shelf above the fridge. "Contains Medication," she wrote in large letters, then peeled it off and stuck it on Jess's bottle.

"That should keep it safe."

Jess laughed. "Thank you."

"How's your husband getting on, love?"

Jess sighed. "Not very well. I'm afraid it's a bit of a struggle."

"In the family?"

"Yeah."

The nurse patted her arm sympathetically. "That's often the way. Hang in there. But if I can give you some advice?"

Jess looked at her.

"Try to make peace with them. Whoever it is. When your husband is dead, you two will be the survivors together…"

Jess breathed out.

Pacing up and down the hall, Jess thought about the nurse's words. She and Myra. An unlikely pair if there ever was one. But it hadn't always been that way. In fact, it had been the opposite for a long time. Myra had looked after her when she'd lost the baby. She'd had Christmas morning with them every year and had helped Jess move into their new house. They'd been friendly, if not friends, right up until Mitch's accident. Until the night the doctors had told them he would probably never wake up.

When she got home, she sat on the porch swing. Then she got up again, pacing around with the handheld phone before she finally worked up the nerve to dial.

Myra answered with a hesitant, "Hello?"

Jess steeled herself.

"I've been thinking that maybe we could meet for coffee."

A pause on the other end. "Coffee?" A sigh. "All right. Why not? Where?"

"I'll meet you at the hospital tomorrow. Around eleven? Then I can spend the afternoon."

"That sounds fine. See you then."

Jess slept better that night than she had since she got back, partly because the exhaustion was definitely catching up with her, but also because she'd finally been able to see her way past the hostility that had been bothering her more than she realized. She'd been unhappy with the situation with Myra for years but hadn't had to face it until now. Alone. With Jil away and the decision to leave her job weighing her down even more. But somehow, even that short conversation with Myra had taken a strain off her mind, and she fell into bed, falling asleep almost immediately.

When the sun creaked over the horizon in the morning, she woke up, turned over, and went back to sleep.

After a few strong cups of coffee, a slow walk through the nature path behind her house, and a long, hot shower, she got dressed and headed to the hospital.

She wondered how many more days she would have to sit here, watching Mitch waste away. Wishing she had the courage to just take him off the machines and let God take him home. But Myra would probably decapitate her, or bar her from his funeral, or both.

And she wondered if she should be angry with Padraig for giving her something else to do or grateful to him for giving her something else to think about. Maybe both.

With half an hour to spare before she met Myra in the lobby, Jess took a tour around the bottom floor, into the gift shop and around the admissions desk.

"Is there a lost and found here?" she asked.

"Have you lost something? It won't be here if it's valuable. It won't even be here if it's not valuable," the person at the desk informed her. What was it with career thieves, Jess wondered. She'd had one at her own school. He'd stolen her ring and pissed off a lot of people, but he'd never even bothered to sell the stuff. He'd just hidden it away like a peculiar little magpie.

The lost and found worker's words needled her.

"Who has access to the lost and found?"

"Everyone. That's why it's out in the open. So people can find lost stuff. Or steal from it, whatever works."

Jess thought about it. What if the thief wasn't interested in selling the goods either? What if they just wanted to take things and grow their own personal hoard?

CHAPTER TWENTY-ONE

The next morning, Jil arrived at the sea aquarium early. Protestors were still marching outside, but she noticed the crowd had thinned a little. She nodded to Ramone as she came in, and he gave her a little salute.

"Lie low this morning," he muttered as she passed. "Something's going on."

Jil kept walking, carrying her briefcase to the office.

Leonard was just coming out.

"Morning," she said.

He smiled. "Hi. Glad to see you didn't get blocked by the picket line."

"I came around the back."

"Good choice."

"You're going out?"

"Sure am."

"Good, before you go, can I get those insurance papers from you? I'm almost finished my report, but I need to make sure I'm not missing anything."

His smile faded a little. "Rebecca checking up on me?" he asked.

Jil shook her head. "No, nothing like that. It's part of the tax assessment." She tried to sound professional and vague at the same time. "The...premiums are part of my calculations."

He nodded, seeming to accept that. "Right. I'm going for the open water exercise. Why don't you come with me, and we can talk about it on the boat? Have you ever been?"

Jil hesitated. She'd been trying to avoid a situation where she could be engaged in conversation about her nonexistent financial skills.

"It would be a good way to see the cost-benefit of proactive health measures," Leonard said.

"How do you mean?"

"Well, the cost of extra trainers and the boat itself is definitely worth the long-term health of the animals. Putting them in the open water and allowing them long-distance swimming keeps them healthier in the long run."

"I see."

"You could see for yourself."

Jil smiled. "Okay, on one condition."

"Sure, what is it?"

"We'll leave work behind and just enjoy the waves."

Leonard smiled. "Sure. We can do that."

"Let me just go check in with Rebecca. I'll be right there."

"Yep. We leave at nine."

"Perfect."

Leonard moved in the direction of the locker rooms, and Jil headed down to the observatory where, by now, she knew she could find Rebecca.

"Walk with me," she said as soon as she saw Jil.

Jil fell into step beside her as she moved up the far side of the underwater observatory and outside, then progressed to the sea lion enclosure. She stopped at the gate to pull against the lock. "Just double-checking," she muttered.

"Why?"

"Didn't you hear?"

"No, I just got here."

"One of the cages was left open last night."

"Did anything escape?"

"No, luckily. But it could have been bad news."

Jil flashed to Ramone's secret enterprise and privately hoped it hadn't been him.

"I'm going on an open water exercise this morning."

Rebecca smiled. "Good. I think you'll enjoy it. Might give you a better idea of what this place is about."

"And it might give me a little opportunity for sleuthing too. Leonard's the only one whose whereabouts I haven't been able to confirm. Except yours."

She hadn't meant to say that so directly, but Rebecca didn't flinch.

"You think I might have murdered my own trainer, caused myself a PR disaster, then hired a PI to find me out?" she said with a sardonic look.

"Stranger things have happened," Jil replied.

Rebecca put a hand on her shoulder. And there it was again, that strange electric jolt sparked by Rebecca's intense gaze that travelled straight through her body, and ended somewhere a lot more sensitive...

"I was at home," she said in a low voice. "Having a glass of red and taking a bath."

"Can anyone confirm that?"

Rebecca's lips pulled upward in a small smirk. "I was... flying solo that night."

Jil's cheeks flushed hot. "I see."

A beeping sound interrupted their conversation. Rebecca stopped and listened, then hurried back across the bridge and down into the whale enclosures.

Tait was rushing up the stairs as they headed down.

"Is that the water level alarm?" Rebecca asked tensely.

Tait turned back around and led them to the source of the noise.

Past the gates, the protestors were pricking up their ears, trying to see over the wall.

"It's Noki and Lulu's tank."

"For fuck's sake," Rebecca muttered.

Jil followed them aboveground and over to the tank that held the other two smaller orcas. They were chattering, their voices sounding distressed, even to Jil's untrained ear. They swam in circles around their tank, the sunlight glinting off the water they splashed into the air.

"Are they just splashing too much water or is there a leak somewhere?"

Jil took in the soaked decks and moved back as one of the whales breeched onto her side, sending another tidal wave crashing over the side.

"What are they doing?"

"Whales are sensitive to noise. She's just showing she doesn't like it."

At least the chanting in the background had been drowned out.

Ramone came rushing down the ramp from the main building.

"I got wind of a problem."

"The water level's low." Jil could see for herself the exposed red segment of the warning yardstick on the side of the tank. The water level was sinking fast.

"Come quick!" Tait rushed back up. Jil hadn't noticed him leave.

"Where?"

"Down below. It's gushing pretty bad."

Ramone got on his walkie-talkie—a scene that was becoming familiar to Jil.

"Repair crews to tank five. *Vite, vite.*"

"Where's the leak?" Rebecca grabbed the young man by the arm.

"It's not a leak. It's the drainpipe. It's wide open."

Rebecca's face blanched. "The drain pipe? Jesus." She looked at Ramone, but he was already hurrying below.

Rebecca jogged behind him and Jil followed, rushing to keep pace with her long strides. All around the park, a loud alarm began firing, like a fire drill or an evacuation warning.

"Wait here," Rebecca said. "I don't want anyone hurt."

She got halfway down the next steps before Ramone gave her a similar warning.

"The boys are getting it closed now. Why don't you just get the water turned on and start filling it back up?"

Rebecca nodded and raced back topside.

"Get that alarm shut off, would you?" she yelled.

The crackling of static, some shouted instructions in Spanish and French, and the blaring over the PA system stopped. The high-pitched beeping from before, however, was still going strong.

"That won't go off until the water level's back up," Rebecca muttered. "Here, help me with this hose."

Jil took the other end of the giant black hose and helped Rebecca drag it to the edge of the tank. The whales swam around, and one stopped to look at her, turning on its side and giving a wave of its pectoral fin.

Jil laughed.

"Don't get too close," Rebecca said. "They're skittish at the moment and they don't know you."

Jil made sure to keep along the fence line as she fed the hose over to the tank.

"Hold it steady. I'm going to turn the water on."

Another trainer, seeing Jil, came rushing through to the deck to help her.

"Thanks, Max," Jil said, recognizing the young man.

"Careful of that pit there," Max said. Jil looked down just in time to avoid stepping in a divot in the concrete. Actually, the whole deck was in need of repair. The tank reminded her of a backyard swimming pool with chipped concrete and blue water.

Suddenly, the hose sputtered and water began to gush out.

Max slipped one end into the side of the tank. "Low budget," he joked.

"We were allocating funds to build a bigger holding tank in the next year," Rebecca said, joining them. "This one used to be fine, but whales grow and the tanks don't."

"At this rate, it will take hours for the water to rise," Max said. "Can we get another set of hoses in?"

"How far have we got to go to get that alarm off?" Rebecca asked aloud.

Max pointed. "There's the line."

Jil followed to where he was pointing.

"Right there," Max said. "That's for the first level alarm. When the water gets that low, an alarm goes off. It dings locally and in the office. If nothing is done, and the water reaches that second line…"

Jil didn't need to hear the rest. She'd heard the blaring alarm that must have been the last warning.

"That one's hardwired into the PA system and can be heard all through the park."

"Does it happen often?"

"On really hot days, we get a lot of evaporation and that can lower the water level. If the whales are playful and splashing a lot, that can impact it too…but it takes a lot to decrease the pool by twenty-five percent. I've never heard the alarm before."

"Yeah, because the drain pipe is not usually left wide open," Rebecca said sarcastically.

Max looked worried. "That can't happen by accident, Rebecca. It takes two overrides to get that thing open."

"What's it for, exactly?" Jil asked.

Max answered. "Once a year at least, this tank has to be completely drained and cleaned. The drain pipe gets fully opened, drains the water, we clean the tank, and then refill it."

"When was the last time the tank was cleaned?"

"Actually, a few weeks ago," Rebecca said. "Maybe it never got shut properly."

Max looked at her doubtfully.

"We've had no problems for ten days and then suddenly it blows? I can't see it."

"A problem with the seal, maybe?"

Max shrugged. "Maybe. Or…"

Rebecca shook her head. "Don't say it, Max."

Jil had been thinking the same thing. Or someone had deliberately tried to drain the tank.

"With two whales inside?" Rebecca said defensively. "Why would anyone try to do that?"

"I don't know, Rebecca, but that observatory was no accident either. Someone's trying to sabotage this place."

CHAPTER TWENTY-TWO

Jess looked up to see Myra getting off the elevator. She stopped in front of Jess, a bit farther away than one would normally greet a member of their family. But at least she wasn't yelling curse words.

"Ready?"

"Yes."

Jess expected them to go through the main doors of the hospital, but instead Myra led her down the corridor and into the women's locker room. She opened a locker and put in her coffee mug, then changed her clothes.

"Since when have you been on staff?" Jess asked.

Myra shrugged. "They had a few extra lockers, so someone offered me one a few years back. They let the volunteers have a place of their own once they've been here long enough. It saves me always having to drag things back and forth from home. Especially in the winter."

Jess looked around, remembering the nurse from her floor with the stolen size nine Skechers.

"Have you ever seen anything suspicious around here, Myra? Like, someone taking things that weren't theirs?"

Myra's eyebrows lifted. "Theft, you mean? No, I've never seen that. Why? Is something missing?"

"More than one something, apparently."

Myra frowned. "That's awful. Who's missing things?"

"The nurses."

"The nurses? Someone's stealing from the nurses? After they've been on their feet twelve hours, looking after sick people? What kind of moral deficit does this person have?"

Jess couldn't help a smile. That feistiness of Myra's was something she hadn't seen in a long time.

"How do you know anyway?"

"One of the nurses mentioned it."

"And they don't know who it is? Don't they have cameras around here?"

Jess stopped. They did. On the outside of the building, in the main lobby, and all the hallways. So the thefts must take place in areas that were not surveilled by CCTV.

"None in here, right?"

"I should hope not," Myra retorted. "We should stake them out."

Jess almost laughed. "And how would we recognize them?"

"Well, by the jewels they're stuffing in their underwear, I guess."

This time Jess did laugh. "I imagine if it's been going on as long as it has, the thief is probably a little more sophisticated than that."

"Right. Probably. How long has it been going on, exactly?"

Jess shrugged. "Years, it seems."

"Years? Well, then they deserve what's coming to them."

Myra struggled out of her shoes and extracted a shoehorn from her locker to help her put on her sensible British style outdoor walking shoes. The same ones she'd had since Jess had met her.

"I'm just going to use the restroom since we're here," Jess said.

Jess leaned on the bathroom stall door to close it. The lock was half off. She thought for a moment. Who could come and go in here? Obviously, more people than she'd thought. Nurses, doctors, volunteers. Even Myra.

Myra wouldn't steal anything—she was far too upstanding for that—but who might?

As she tried to wash her hands, she discovered that two of the sinks were, indeed, broken. Not only broken but turned off instead of repaired. Shameful.

She washed her hands at one of the working sinks and headed out the door with Myra.

Jess stepped out into the street and felt the sun unexpectedly hit her skin.

"Could it be that spring has finally decided to come?" Myra said at her side.

She led the way down the street. "There's a nice café here. They make homemade muffins."

Jess smiled. Myra had never been much of a baker, though she'd tried.

"You can get a good old-fashioned cup of tea, without three layers of hot soya foam and syrups that spike your glucose."

A good old-fashioned cup of tea sounded great right about now. Whether it was the long days in the hospital, or the nights alone at home, or the relief of finally having told Mitch everything that she'd never been able to say to him, she felt a hollow fatigue like she'd never experienced before. Something that coffee wouldn't be able to touch.

She followed Myra into the café and stood admiring the paintings on the wall. It was definitely an artsy place—probably an even split between a gallery and a coffee shop, and not the sort of venue she'd expect Myra to go to often. But as she saw her mother-in-law carrying a pot of tea and a sieve to the table, she understood. Each tabletop held a bowl of raw sugar cubes, dainty milk and cream servers, and a rack of mugs. Just like a kitchen.

Jess slowly walked along the rows of paintings and back to the table where Myra was swirling the pot.

She paused by a sculpture and her heart sped up.

"You know these artists?" Myra said, watching her.

"Just that one. There."

Jess pointed to the sculpture—almost laser cut, a woman's bust and partial torso, ending at the neck.

"Talented."

"She is, yes."

Myra eyed her curiously. "Are you going to tell me or do I have to ask?"

Could it be that she'd known all along?

"We used to see each other," Jess said quietly.

Myra only nodded. "I see. How long did you...see each other?"

"Not long. I wasn't...exciting enough for her, I think."

Myra poured Jess a mugful. "Yes, well, excitement is overrated, sometimes. Loyalty and devotion are much more important and virtuous." She stopped. "I didn't mean it like that."

"But you do blame me," Jess said. She had no energy left for a fight, and her words came out flat. Facts instead of accusations.

"No. I blame myself."

Jess looked up.

"What for?"

"Because I think I knew you two weren't right for each other and I didn't give him a way out when he asked. I reminded him...I reminded him of his vows before God. Of his duty. Even when he told me he was unhappy. That you didn't love him."

"I did love him," Jess said.

"I know. But not...in that way."

Jess stirred a cube of sugar into her tea, more for something to do than because she actually wanted it. But watching it dissolve on her spoon gave her something to focus on.

"I didn't know, when I married him. I didn't know there would be a Lily out there."

"But you're not...with her anymore."

"No."

"Are you…with someone else?"

Jess nodded. "Yes."

"Can I ask her name?"

Jess looked up and saw for the first time how much Myra had aged these past few years. No longer as quick, nor as judgmental, it would seem. She would have expected a scoff at least. Women didn't belong with women.

But she got none of that.

"Jil," she answered.

Myra poured milk in her tea thoughtfully. "And are you happy together?"

Jess smiled. "Most of the time."

"Yes, well…that's a relationship for you. I'm…I'm sorry, Jessica. You didn't deserve my anger. You deserved my love."

Jess felt the tears spill over before she even knew she was going to cry. "I'm sorry too. I'm sorry I couldn't love him the way he wanted. The way he deserved. It's just…it's not in me."

"I see that now. I realize what a struggle it must have been, knowing you as I know you. I…I should have counseled him differently. I should have…I should have done a lot of things differently. Forgive me, Jessica." Myra put her hand over Jess's and smiled sadly. "I can't tell him, so I'll tell you."

"Life would be easier if we could get along, wouldn't it?"

"Yes. Of course it would be. But there are things…"

"Let's not talk about it right now."

She was too tired. She couldn't fight about anything else.

Myra seemed to understand that and tactfully changed the subject. "I'm curious, tell me about your job. What are you doing now if you're not at school?"

"Actually, I'm still sorting it out, but at the moment, I'm trying to figure out who the thief is at the hospital."

"Really? Like a detective?"

"A PI," Jess said. The words felt strange on her tongue. A private investigator was not something she'd ever thought she'd be.

"Oh. Well, that's an unexpected turn. How did you learn anything about that?"

"Jil," Jess said shyly. "She's a PI. And a very good one. Her boss, Padraig, he's about to retire, and since she's away..."

"Is she? Away?"

"Yes. In the Caribbean. We were there together, but I had to come back..."

Myra's face fell. "For Mitch. You came back from your vacation?"

"They called to tell me he was declining, so I...I got the next plane out."

"And how did Jil react?"

"She got me on the plane. But I'm afraid I didn't stop to think about her much. I'm afraid I might not be very good at relationships, actually, now that I'm looking at everything."

Myra patted her hand. "We all learn, dear. Nobody's perfect."

"So anyway, her boss is shorthanded with her being away, and the hospital director is a friend of his, so he said he'd look into it."

"So he roped you in."

Jess laughed. "Sort of, yes."

Myra sipped her tea. "Right. Well, I'm sure you'll do it if you set your mind to it."

Jess welcomed the mental switch. It was a relief after the drab days and nights of mint green walls and solo swings on the porch.

"You haven't heard any rumors, have you?"

"No. Not at all. Though I didn't know there were any questions to ask on the subject so I'm afraid I didn't pay attention to that."

"It's odd. The thefts only take place on certain days of the week, but most of the staff at the hospital work shift work. They aren't reliably in on any given day."

"Yes, and some of them, it seems, are in almost every day. Overtime, double duty, it's quite something to observe."

"What about food servers?"

"Food servers?"

"Yes, wouldn't they have access to the building? They bring food to every room, don't they?"

Myra frowned. "Yes, but they have their own staff room on the bottom floor. They don't share the locker room with the nurses and doctors."

"So who do you know who's only in on a Monday?"

Myra frowned. "Well, apart from the chaplain…"

"The chaplain is in on a Monday?" Jess frowned. He seemed an unlikely suspect.

"He runs a volunteer prayer circle and helps organize the volunteers. Knitting boots and hats for the newborns, prayer circles for patients, and anything else that passes through the doors of the chapel, really."

Jess sighed. "Okay. Servicemen are too conspicuous. And infrequent. And half the thefts have taken place in or around the locker room."

"Any particular floor?"

"Yes. The one Mitch is on, as it happens. As well as one other wing."

"Which one?"

"NICU."

Myra frowned.

"What?"

She shook her head. "No. It's probably not connected. At least I would seriously hope not.

"What?"

"Well…there's another prayer circle that meets on that wing on Mondays in the chapel—a set series of prayers for the babies in the NICU. Some of the volunteers are baby holders a few or more days a week."

Before she could ask any more questions, Jess's phone beeped with a message.

"What?" said Myra, seeing Jess's face.

She jumped up.

"C'mon, we have to go."

"What's happening?"

"It's the hospital. Mitch is coding."

CHAPTER TWENTY-THREE

R eady?" Leonard led the way to the boat. Jil watched him climb steadily over and in. No hesitation. She was impressed with the prosthetic and kept looking at the design, which made the leg look more like a motorcycle than a limb.

"Special issue," Leonard said as she sat down.

"What is?"

"The leg."

Jil blushed, hoping he hadn't thought she was staring.

"How long have you had it?"

"This leg?"

"Or any leg…"

He laughed. "This one's a couple years old. I got my first at age seven when my dad was in a car wreck with me in the back seat."

Jil looked at him. "And the shark story…?"

He pulled down the top of his wetsuit to show a scar that ran over the shoulder blade and up over the collarbone.

"Yikes."

"Yeah. Almost put me out of business for good. That's when I went back and finished my accounting license."

"Right. I guess shark diving isn't for everyone. Long-term, I mean."

Leonard didn't look at her as he sat down. "Or even short-term. It can screw you up for life."

He yanked the outboard motor and it revved up. "Ready?" he shouted over the waves.

"Let's go."

He stood up and waved to the trainers at the gates and started putting slowly forward. Jil watched in fascination as two bottlenose dolphins popped up behind the boat and began surfing their wake. They headed out to sea, the dolphins keeping a close pace. It seemed like the boat tour went on forever, but the dolphins didn't slow down. They could swim hard.

"How do you know where to go, or how far?"

Leonard pointed. "The buoys here. They mark the end of the sea aquarium's routes.

"I would miss them if I didn't know they were there. They seem so random."

"You have to know where to look."

Jil took note of the large orange buoys, large enough for someone to stand on.

The dolphins seemed to recognize them too, because one bonked it playfully with its nose, then turned around and started leading the boat back toward the aquarium.

"They jump so high," Jil said in amazement.

"Wait till you're in the water with them."

"What?"

Suddenly, he shoved her and she fell off the side of the boat, whacking her arm so hard on the side that her head began to spin. Water churned beside her, cold and dark. Even in the Caribbean the sea was cold this far out. And dangerous.

The waves were large and tumultuous. They swept up under the boat, rocking it and crashing over her.

She fought to remain topside, but she was getting tossed about in the waves. She looked back toward shore but couldn't even see the bay. They were a long way out. She reached back for the boat and tried to haul herself up. But he kicked her hand away and she yelped.

"Sorry," he called. "I tried to save you, but I couldn't get my damn metal leg off in time before you went under."

Jesus. He'd planned this. Why hadn't she seen this coming?

He leaned closer, mocking her.

"You shouldn't have insisted on swimming with dolphins. They're wild animals, you know. And how was I supposed to know you could barely swim?"

Jil sputtered and kicked as another wave carried her up and over its crest. At least it hadn't crashed over her. Maybe if she faced out and saw them coming, she could ride them instead of drown in them.

The motor revved and he took off, sending a giant wake up and over her. She felt panic setting in. How the hell was she going to get back to shore? With no life vest, no direction, and an injured arm, she would definitely die.

Her breathing got shallow, rapid.

What am I going to do? What am I going to do?

She fought the sea as it tried to drag her to its bottom. Her arm was sore from where she'd bashed it against the boat, and the fingers on the other hand were crushed from Leonard's stomp. The pain alone would be enough to keep her awake, but she needed to swim.

Why bother? She'd never make it. She was going to die.

No, you will not.

Her shoes were pulling her under. All it would take was a few good kicks to get them off. She shoved them off her feet, and once they fell away, it got easier to stay afloat. She remembered Max's words and went a little more horizontal, thanking God the waves weren't worse. Her arms felt like pins and needles from the wrist to the shoulder.

Suddenly, something bumped her from the side.

A shark. A shark had found her already. She was going to be eaten.

The water beside her splashed, and a dome head with bright eyes popped up out of the water, chittering.

"Koko?"

Another splash to her left made her whip around. There was Relay.

Jil wasn't sure whether to laugh or cry. Captive dolphins, out on the open ocean, and her, stranded.

Koko bobbed her head and swam in a circle around Jil. Had they come back for her, or come back to drown her? She didn't know much about dolphins, but she knew they were wild animals, despite being domesticated. Still, she reached out and touched Koko's smooth back. Koko stopped and waited. She lined up next to Jil like she'd done at the tank.

"No way. I can't," Jil said.

The dolphin lifted her head and nosed Jil in the shoulder.

How else did she expect to get back in? There wasn't exactly a fleet of lifeboats out here.

Tentatively, Jil put her hands on Koko's dorsal fin, and the dolphin took off.

She got five meters before she went under.

Relay bumped her back to the surface and Koko tried again. This time, Jil was ready for the forward lurch and managed to hold on a little longer—not bad for a beginner, and certainly better than she'd done in the lagoon. She couldn't believe she was riding a dolphin. Her arm hurt like a bitch, but riding a dolphin ranked right up there with the coolest experiences in her life.

Koko surfaced and swam around her, doing her Zeus move. Jil was still fighting to stay afloat in the waves, but having the dolphins for company was making her panic a lot less.

She caught hold of Koko's dorsal fin and put her head down, preparing for the lightning bolt of the takeoff. Koko streaked through the water, riding the waves as Jil did her best not to drown and not to let go. The pain in her arm was excruciating, but she held on, and held on, until finally she was riding the waves and not fighting them.

Koko came up for air, and Jil rode with her.

And then she fell off again.

But this time, when she looked up, she could see the sea aquarium in the distance.

"Look at that, girl," Jil sputtered. Her arms were aching. Her body was cold and heavy. But seeing the sea aquarium gave her renewed hope.

"Okay, let's go again."

But suddenly, Koko took off, swimming in the opposite direction from the sea aquarium.

"Hey! Come back!"

Jil was sapped. She could barely keep afloat. The open water swimming and the strength it had taken to keep holding on had taken its toll on her, and she coughed, feeling herself going under more with each wave. Relay swam around Jil, pushing her arm up toward the surface. Jil tried to go horizontal and Relay prodded her—in encouragement or out of training, Jil couldn't tell.

When a large wave almost took her under, Relay pushed her up on his back, chittering.

She thought about trying to swim for shore, but she could barely tread water.

Then she heard the thunder. A fork of lightning flashed out in the direction Koko had swum and her heart skipped.

When had the sky gotten so dark?

A low rumbling across the water grew closer and closer.

"Hey! Hey! Jil!"

Someone was yelling. She looked around, but another wave got her and she went under. Relay pushed her up and she coughed, and gasped.

When she popped up again, she saw Max leaning over the side of a motorboat, led by Koko, who swam around them, chittering and rolling over.

Strong hands yanked Jil out of the water and into the boat. She landed on the hull and puked up sea water and what was left of her lunch.

"Nice. What the hell happened?" said Max. He threw a towel over her and she took it, shivering. "Leonard said you dove in after the dolphins and wouldn't come in. Then you started drowning. What the fuck?"

Jil puked again and put her head down between her legs. "Fake news," she managed.

Max helped her up onto a seat.

"He pushed me in."

"What?" Rebecca said from the back of the boat. "He pushed you in? Why would he do that?"

In the water, the two dolphins popped their heads up, looking over the side of the boat.

"Your guess is as good as mine," Jil said. "I'm pretty sure I've never done anything to piss him off. So maybe he figured out who I was and has something to hide. That's my best guess."

"Good work, guys," Max called.

"You got a fish?" Jil asked.

Max laughed. "I always have fish."

He dug into the side cooler.

"Make it a big one."

He gave her two of the choicest offerings, and she turned to the open water to hand-feed them to the dolphins. She could barely see the animals through her tears. "You're the best," she choked.

Max patted her arm. "Made some new friends, I see. Did you catch a ride?"

Jil smiled, swiping her nose with the back of her hand. "Oh, you'd have been so proud of the way I fell off, and fell off, and fell off."

"I'm just impressed they came back for you. Must be one special girl."

Rebecca revved the motor, getting ready to steer them back to shore. "Let's get in. There's a storm coming. And I want to hear everything on the way."

The gray clouds were rolling in with alarming speed, and the wind had definitely picked up.

Koko gave her that same smiling look and dove back down, leading the way home.

Back at the sea aquarium, people had assembled on the breakers. Someone ran up to the highest point and waved. The people farther up were waiting at the gates to let in the dolphins and the boats that were spread out on the water. Rebecca had radioed in that they'd found Jil and now everyone could head on home.

Koko and Relay dove down and through the passage to their lagoon as Rebecca docked their craft.

Jil was met with a thermos of hot chocolate and another set of towels.

"We've set up the electric blanket inside," Tait said, jumping into the boat to help Jil get out. She was surprised to find she could barely stand up. Her head felt woozy, and the strength was gone from her legs. Just as she was about to go down, Max grabbed her from behind and scooped her up.

"C'mon, rookie. Let's go."

CHAPTER TWENTY-FOUR

W hat's happening?"
Jess burst through the door, and the whine of the machines caught her ear.

"Everyone clear."

A whine and a crack. Mitch's torso jumped off the bed.

"Oh, God."

A nurse took her by the elbow and moved her out of the way. "He's gone into cardiac arrest. They're trying to resuscitate him."

Jess looked up to see Myra pacing the hallway.

She fled out the door. "Myra, we have to tell them to stop."

"Sinus."

She looked through the door. The machine was counting out his heartbeats.

Myra looked stricken. Her face had gone pale. Like she was about to faint. She hovered on the doorstep while the doctor waited at the bedside with his paddles in the air. But the monitor kept beating.

"Go for a walk," the nurse said. "You don't want to see this. Go now."

Myra stumbled away from the door and Jess did her best to keep up with her down the hallway.

"Myra? Where are you going?"

"The chapel."

Without another word, Jess followed Myra, who moved with extraordinary speed for a woman her age. But when Myra outstripped her down the hall and had to turn around, she looked surprised.

"Are you not well, Jessica?"

Jess shook her head. "No."

"They'll set him right. He'll be fine. He's always fine." Myra's hands on the wall railing were shaking.

"It's not that. It's me. Sorry."

"What's the matter, dear?"

"Rheumatoid arthritis."

Myra's eyebrows shot up.

"Shall I slow down a bit?"

Jess kept walking. "Thanks."

They were nearly there. She could see the glow of the blue stained glass windows down the hall.

And, as usual, the chapel was empty.

Myra sank down into the nearest pew. Jess reached into her purse and found a mint at the bottom. "Here. Might help."

"Thank you. That was terrible. I had no idea...what I was asking. What I was putting him through."

Jess sat beside her. "We don't have to. We can make it stop."

Myra took a rosary from the back of the bench and started moving it between her fingers, almost like a worry stone. She didn't say anything for a long moment.

"I've been thinking. About what you said. About Mitch being able to see us and hear us. About being in pain." She pressed her hanky to her nose. She was the only woman Jess knew who carried one, and it was always with her.

"I shouldn't have said those things—"

"No. You were right."

"So harshly," Jess finished.

Myra nodded. "Yes, well...I'm beginning to think that maybe I haven't been listening to anybody lately. Even the Lord himself.

My ears have been clogged. And I'm sorry, Jessica. It's a terrible thing to watch your child…"

"Yeah. I can see that."

"But I haven't been alone on the journey, as you have been. And I know we haven't always agreed, but I should have reached out to you instead of making you my enemy. It was unchristian of me. It was…it was wrong. I had my people and you didn't, and I'm sorry."

"I'm glad for you. That you had your prayer group."

"They've been with me through some very difficult times. Even the ones who didn't know Mitch."

Jess looked at her. "Didn't know Mitch? Don't they all know him?"

Myra frowned. "Most of them, yes. They're mostly members of my church. But a few joined over the years. One, I met here. She's a volunteer."

"And you're worried about how they would take it? If we decided…"

Myra breathed out heavily. "Yes, if we decided to let him go. I'd have to explain it to them. I'm afraid that's what I've been dithering over more than anything else. Seeming to lose faith. Though I don't even know why I'm worried about it. It's that Mary-Ann, mostly. The one who joined a few years ago."

"The one who doesn't know Mitch?"

Myra looked at her. "Yes."

Jess nodded. Something niggled at the back of her mind, but she couldn't focus on it. The sound of her own thoughts whirling in her brain was overwhelming. She felt like she was going to faint.

The whine and the thud. The crack of his chest.

Myra took a breath. "It's time. You're right. We're letting him suffer and it's not fair. If you're ready, and if we pray about it, I think it's time now."

Jess felt the weight of her word land like rocks.

Time to let him go.

Yes. It was time.

Jess went blindly down the hall, searching out a nurse.

"Can I help?"

"Yes. I need Dr. Rabinovitch. And we need those papers." She didn't recognize her own voice. Quiet. Sure.

"Yes. Of course. I'll find him." She quickly headed off down the hall.

A few moments later, the doctor met them in Mitch's room.

"You're sure?" he said.

And it was Myra who answered. "I should have listened a long time ago, Doctor. We're sure."

Jess sat and read over the folder for what felt like the one hundredth time. Signing the papers was painful. Physically, in her hands and the way they cramped, but also in her chest, her stomach, her lungs. It felt like everything was pressing on her, suffocating her.

She handed the folder back.

"Okay. I'll file this."

"Can we do it this afternoon, Doctor? I want Myra's prayer group to have a chance to get here."

Myra squeezed her shoulder.

"Yes, by all means."

Her legs were shaking as she got up, but Myra took hold of her elbow. "Steady, dear."

Jess held Mitch's hand for another moment before she kissed his forehead and left. She badly needed to get outside, into the fresh air, and take a few breaths before she screamed.

The wind was back, rushing through the courtyard, but she was glad about it. It was bracing enough to whip her in the face and dry the tears that wouldn't stop falling. Yes, it was the right thing to do. Yes, it was time. But God, what an ending.

She wandered through the gardens, stopping to look at the crocuses that had just started to bloom. Little buds of spring, shoving their way up to the sunlight.

She fingered the ferns, smelled the cedar trees, anything to ground her into this time and place.

And then she turned and went back inside.

When she arrived at the door to Mitch's room, a group of women stood in the hallway.

Myra came out and was immediately surrounded.

"Thank you for coming."

"Of course we came."

"Myra, I know it's not my business to interfere..."

Jess stopped and looked as a smaller woman with white hair led Myra a short distance from the group. When Jess looked closer, she realized that the woman wasn't as old as she looked. Her hair was white as swan's feathers, but her skin was smooth, and she wore thick glasses.

She couldn't hear what they were whispering, but she could guess from the way Myra's shoulders were tightening.

Another member of the group approached and took Myra back.

"C'mon, now."

They led her inside.

Jess watched the other woman closely. She turned around, saw Jess, and came toward her and smiled. Sort of.

"Hi, I'm Mary-Ann."

Oh. Mary-Ann. The career prayer.

"Jessica."

"You're Mitch's wife?"

Whatever she might have said next was cut off as Dr. Rabinovitch walked toward her down the hall. "The priest is on his way. I called him myself."

"Thank you."

When she looked up next, Mary-Ann had slipped away.

She watched from the doorway as the rest of the women stood in a circle in the corner. Myra beckoned to her and she slipped in, sank into her rocking chair in the corner, and waited for the incense and oil, the last rites, and the final blessings.

"How long will it take?" she whispered to Dr. Rabinovitch.

He shrugged. "Hours or days. Depending."

Jess sank into a chair. She didn't have the energy in her for days.

The nurses came in and removed the IV from Mitch's arm, then disconnected his feeding tube. They took the pads off his chest, turned off the machines, and wheeled out the pole. They dimmed the lights on their way out, and he was left looking as peaceful as if he were only sleeping. Amazing what a difference it made, all the equipment, and how normal he looked now without it.

For a second, Jess was gripped by a horrible feeling that she was letting a healthy man die. That stripped of all this hospital gear, he was just dreaming, about to wake up any moment.

But then the group of women started praying softly. The Hail Mary. The Lord's Prayer. She fell into the chant of the familiar words, which still held more comfort in them, more routine and certainty, than she would ever have imagined.

When the last prayer was over, one of the women began to sing a hymn. One she recognized from every summer Mass she'd ever attended. A reminder that spring would come again, one day.

She looked over and saw Myra gripping the hands of the women next to her in the circle.

Singing Mitch home.

It was past two o'clock in the morning and the phone was buzzing.

Before Jess even answered, she knew what news it would bring. Nobody else would call at this hour. And the heaviness in her body had been warning her all night.

Two seventeen a.m.

She imagined getting up, getting dressed, and getting confronted with the fight of her life. Should she get in the ring? Did she even have the right, anymore?

"Are they still there?"

"They've been here since last night. He's had someone by his side all the time."

She let out a breath. "Thank you."

Jess looked at her wedding ring on the side of the bed, held in the box she'd originally received it in. What would she do with it? Would she just bury it in the bottom of a drawer somewhere? Sell it for charity? Put it in his coffin?

With a heavy sigh, Jess leaned back on the pillow and stared out the window. The crescent moon was a mere sliver over the elm tree in her front yard, the sky a starless black.

The morning would dawn without Mitch in it.

After a few moments, she got up, got dressed again, and went to say good-bye.

❖

"I'm sorry for your loss."

They handed Jess the bag that contained the final items that she had left: his shaving kit, his wedding ring, his comb. She tucked it into her bag and left the nurses' station, past the door to the room where Mitch had lain sleeping for the past five years.

The bed was stripped. Remade. Tight hospital corners and a single pillow. They should burn the mattress, used as it was. Air out the room. Cast some sort of spell to remove the ghosts and cobwebs of all the guilt and past conversations.

But someone else would move in there, like he'd never been there at all.

Tears began to flow down her face and she couldn't stop them.

She ducked into the locker room, into the stall and sat on the toilet seat, weeping.

For a few minutes, she sat, pressing a tissue to her face, then she ran a cold stream of water to splash over her nose and eyes. It was only when she reached for the paper towel and caught sight of the u-bend that she thought of it. Something was sticking out of the PVC attachment. She squinted. A tiny piece of gold chain.

Why not? What better hiding place than inside the bathroom itself?

She bent down to examine the plumbing and popped the u-bend right off. A necklace fell onto the floor, followed by a ring. She tipped the piece of PVC over in her hand. It all fell out.

"Jackpot."

Quickly, she replaced it all, snapped the PVC piece back into place, and dialed Padraig.

"I think I've solved your case."

"You're kidding."

"No, I'm not. I've found the stash, and I have a pretty good idea who it belongs to."

"Can you wait there?"

"For a few minutes, yes. Mitch died last night, and I'm heading home."

"So sorry to hear it, Jessica. My condolences. I'll get someone there as soon as I can."

Within ten minutes, the police were in the locker room with her.

"Hey!" Morgan, Jil's old friend from the police force, slapped her on the back. "How are you? Long time, no see."

She returned his hug. "And look, another crime scene." She smiled ironically.

The first time she'd seen Morgan had been when she was principal of St. Marguerite's. The last time had been some sort of retirement party and he'd had a few too many hard lemonades.

"What did you find here?"

"Oh, you know, a good old stash of goods."

"Souvenirs?"

"Apparently. Though some of them are pretty valuable, so I don't understand why she wouldn't have sold them."

"Sometimes it's better to wait," Morgan said. "They can be offloaded six months, a year later, when things have cooled down. And it's also pretty smart not to have taken them home with her. I'd say this is probably a career thief."

"Yeah, I've met a few of those. I seem to attract them in my life."

"Maybe you're meant to be a PI."

She winked at him. "You never know."

An hour later, Jess and Zeus were seated in the living room, watching the breaking news clip. Zeus's giant head was in Jess's lap and he kept turning his face to look at her.

"Missed you too, you giant suck."

He burrowed in and pawed her leg.

"A long-standing problem at the Rockford Memorial Hospital has finally been solved. Former volunteer and prayer meeting coordinator Mary-Ann Beecham has been charged with theft and concealment of private property. She is accused of stealing from the staff and patients of our downtown hospital for years. A citizen tipped off investigators earlier today, and several hundred items of stolen property were found and returned to their owners. Other pieces are still awaiting collection. If you think an item of yours might have been taken from Rockford Memorial, you are asked to call police to file a report."

Chapter Twenty-five

When Jil woke up, she was lying in the semi-lit staff room, cocooned in a blanket with the air conditioning on full blast. Low voices came from across the room, and for a moment, she just lay still, listening.

"No word yet?"

"No. Carole says patrols have been out all afternoon and there's no sign of him."

"What was he thinking? What were we thinking, believing him like that? It's obvious now…"

"I know, I know. But he was pretty upset about having to leave her there. We should've—"

"Yeah, remembered that we'd seen him toss off his leg in three seconds flat? He could've saved her if he'd wanted to."

"And the way he took off out of here, like a bat outta hell."

"Exactly. I wish I'd thought to stop him. I was just…"

"I know. Me too. We all were just focused on getting the boat on the water."

"How far can you get on a Sea-Doo?"

"Far enough," Jil said, sitting up. "Especially if you have help."

Rebecca and Ramone looked up from their conversation, and Ramone got up from the table.

"Hi. Glad to see you're alive."

"Takes more than a bullet to stop this train." She winked.

He grinned. "That's a good one. Here." He handed her a glass of water and she gulped it down.

"Thanks."

For a second, nobody spoke. Jil took note of her throbbing hand, her aching arm, and the empty, hollow feeling in her gut from having retched up seawater.

"Now that you're awake, Carole is going to have a few questions for you," Rebecca said.

Jil leaned back on the couch. Her legs still felt like jelly. And she wished Jess was here.

"Tell me what happened," Jil said.

Rebecca looked at her, confused. "What do you mean? We should be asking that of you!"

"No, when Leonard came back here."

Ramone and Rebecca exchanged a look. Ramone bowed his head. "He came through here like a storm in a teacup, yelling to everyone that you'd fallen out of the boat. That you drowned. And the dolphins were on the lam."

"So naturally everyone panicked," Rebecca said, shaking her head. "We got crews together. Got everyone out on the water looking for you and for the dolphins. We turned around to get Leonard to point us in the right direction. Tell us where you were at exactly when you fell out of the boat. Then we realized he was gone."

"Like a bat out of hell," Ramone added.

"We didn't even see him go. Didn't have time to think to send anyone looking for him," said Rebecca. "So we all flanked out. Then by the time we figured it out, he was gone."

"So sorry, Jil." Ramone patted her shoulder. "We should've clued in faster. It was just—"

"Hey, don't be sorry," Jil said. "It must have been a total shock. Which is exactly how he planned it to be. Now, the only question is, what the hell is he covering up, and why? That's my first priority to figure out."

"Um, no," Rebecca said. "Your first priority is to go home and get some rest. And some food. And a hot bath."

"And maybe a drink on the beach, which is what St. Emeline is all about," Ramone added.

"Actually, you're going to come home with me tonight," Rebecca said in a way that didn't invite any discussion.

Jil let out a deep breath. "Okay," she said. Besides, it would be easier to work out the details with other people than all alone in her head. "Ramone, you're coming too. And Max."

Rebecca nodded. "Yes, that's a good idea. We'll order pizza and make those margaritas Ramone was talking about."

Rebecca pulled the open-topped Jeep through a gate that closed automatically behind them. She maneuvered up a steep white driveway and into a porte cochere.

"Wow," Jil breathed under her breath. Rebecca's beach house was a mansion.

Ramone looked at her and opened his eyes wide.

Jil hopped out of the front seat and Max pulled up behind them in his own beat-up four-door.

"Nice pad, Rebecca," he said, whistling.

She rolled her eyes. "Thanks. Bought when property values here hadn't yet skyrocketed. C'mon in."

They sat around on the porch, looking down on the open water.

"Look. Another bust-cum-theft," Max said dryly.

Jil watched as a harbor master's boat made contact with a bigger vessel.

"Is corruption a big problem here?" she asked.

Rebecca snorted. "It's a joke," she said. "Half the harbor masters are on the take, from what Carole tells me. The gendarme spend half their time investigating real crime and the other half trying to figure out which of the authorities are squirreling away the merchandise."

"Nice," Jil said.

"It's hard to blame some of them," Ramone put in. "St. Emeline is a poor country. A lot of the people live in poverty. Even the ones who are working. I knew a guy. He told me he made ten times as much smuggling as he did at the job he had. And he only kept the job so he wasn't busted for smuggling."

"Any word from Carole?" Max asked.

Rebecca put down her phone she'd been checking and shook her head. "Nothing. No sign of him."

"Where the hell could he have gone?" Ramone said. "He's just vanished into the wind. Do you think he got off the island?"

"How? He couldn't have gotten on a plane. They were at the airport. He'd have had to have gotten on a boat."

"Or disappeared into a cabin or a house somewhere," Jil mused. "It's unlikely that he planned this. So probably he didn't exactly have an escape plan."

Just then, her phone buzzed with an incoming video call. "Hey," she said softly.

"Hey," said Jess. "You're alive? I talked to Rebecca."

She ducked out to the porch. "I am. Though I did swallow half the ocean."

"So where are you now? Where is this lunatic? Are they going to catch him or what?"

"I'm at Rebecca's house. The police thought maybe he'd come to my place looking for me if he found out I didn't drown."

"Right," Jess said tensely.

She looked like she hadn't slept for days, Jil noted.

"Have you been to the hospital?"

"Yes. I'm going straight to the funeral home tomorrow morning."

"So sorry, love."

"Me too. I wish I could be there with you."

"Same. I'm just going to get done with this case ASAP and get home."

"Good. Okay, let's get on with that goal. I've been thinking about that insurance issue you brought up. Then I did a little more digging."

"Well, I think that's what set him off, finally. I asked him for the documents just as we were heading out on the water. He probably figured out who I was and didn't want me asking any more questions."

"That's what I think too. Luckily, Rebecca is a pretty good sleuth and found the documents. She sent them to me while you were sleeping."

Jil headed back inside and grabbed a slice of the pizza that had just arrived. She was suddenly starving.

"Were you talking to my girlfriend?"

Rebecca blushed. "Your phone was ringing. I answered it."

Ramone moved over to make room for her to sit back down. She put the phone on the table and they all crowded in to talk to Jess.

"Hi, everyone." She ran a hand through her hair.

"Sorry. Didn't mean to put you on the spot."

"No, it's fine. Nice to see you, Ramone."

"Hi."

"So what do you think?" Rebecca asked. "I feel like an idiot, but this was Leonard's department, not mine."

"Insurance isn't for everyone," Jess said.

"Numbers are Jess's thing," Jil said. "She'd have been much better suited to this cover than I was."

Rebecca smiled. "Well, at least one of us is on the ball."

"It's a pretty basic policy," Jess said. "I mean, as basic as you can get for a sea aquarium. But it's not a motive for murder."

"But why did he have it in the first place?" Rebecca asked. "We have insurance on the aquarium through the business. I don't understand why he needed a separate policy."

"Yeah, I saw that. Tell me if we've got all this right. The sea aquarium is insured for ten million."

Rebecca nodded. "Like, fire, flood, acts of God you mean?"

"Yes, and also catastrophic business loss."

"Okay."

"I've never heard of that," Jil said.

"I've only seen it a few times. Or a variation of it," Jess said. "It's not really surprising. This insurance company specializes in terms of operations and commodities. A lot of these policies are tailor-made for large corporations."

"Of course," Jil answered. "Not everybody needs loss of life insurance on their dolphins."

"Exactly. You can get an insurance policy for anything, really, as long as you have an insurer willing to accept the risk."

"But Leonard's policy is something specific. It's only on the whale. And not only on the life of the whale, but also a rider on its ability to perform."

Jil exhaled slowly. "Okay. So, if it got injured or refused to do its routine?"

"Right. Or if word got out that your prize whale ate a trainer and couldn't be in shows anymore?"

Jess nodded. "I'd say that qualified."

"I don't get it, though. The only people who would know the terms of the policy—and benefit from them—are the owners. And why would Leonard want to shut down his own business? Surely he'd make more money than that over the long term."

Jess shrugged. "Wanting all the money at once? Wanting to cover something up?"

Jil thought for a moment.

"Embezzlement?" she said.

"I was thinking the same thing," said Rebecca.

"That's what I suspected," Jess said.

Jil waited while she riffled through the papers.

"Everything makes sense," Jess said. "The whale's life was insured for a million dollars."

"What? That can't be right," Rebecca said. "It was only half a million to buy."

"Right, but that doesn't take into account the loss of income over the long term. Which is what the policy covered."

"It seems like double insurance."

"Kind of. But you can insure the contents of your house and also insure an expensive piece of jewelry separately. There's no reason you can't do the same on something like this. There aren't any special qualifications to take out insurance on something. You only have to prove you'd be out of pocket with a loss."

"And since Leonard negotiated the purchase of the whale, he took out insurance on it without me knowing. God. I'm so stupid."

"No, not stupid. It was a bold move."

"So that's why he's been trying to kill my whale. So he can collect his money."

"Yes."

"Asshole."

"Did he have these policies on all the whales?"

"Yes, but the other ones were insured for a lot less." Jess squinted down at some numbers.

Jil remembered the breach in the tank of the smaller sisters. He could have collected a two-for-one there.

"Okay, so now we know why he wanted to kill the whales. We just don't know why he needed the money."

Rebecca yawned. "Do you mind if we try to figure it out in the morning? I want a plate of appetizers, a stiff martini, and a good night's sleep."

"We see eye to eye," said Ramone. "Minus the martini. I'd like a beer."

"I'm signing off too," Jess said. "For much the same, but with wine."

"I'll call you later," Jil promised.

Later, when everyone had gone to bed, she texted Jess.

Skype?

Almost immediately, her tablet began to ding. Jess's face popped up on the screen. In the dim lamplight, she looked gorgeously disheveled, and Jil felt a stab of homesickness.

"How's the funeral planning going?"

Jess ran a hand through her hair. "Done, really. Myra already had most of it sorted. Funny, though, we really had no idea what he wanted. We'd never talked about it."

"Why would you?" Jil said quietly.

"There was this one song he mentioned, though..."

"How does it go?"

"You know I can't sing," Jess protested.

"Which is strange, since you play so well."

Jess chuckled. "Well, that's where the talent ends."

"Do you know 'His Eye is on the Sparrow'?"

Jil sang the opening bars, and Jess's jaw dropped.

"That's quite a voice."

"Ha. Yeah right," Jil said shortly. "Haven't sung since I was a kid. But I know that hymn."

"From *Sister Act*?" Jess guessed. "That's where Mitch heard it. He said to me specifically—sing that at my funeral."

"That's probably where I heard it later, but my mother used to sing it to me as a bedtime lullaby." She looked down, away, trying to look back into her past for a moment.

"I think Mitch might have had a bit of a crush on Lauryn Hill," Jess confessed.

"Who didn't?" Jil exhaled softly, her shoulders slumping forward as she brought her face closer to the screen. "I wish I could be there with you tonight."

Jess smiled through the tears. "I know. And I wish you were here too."

When they hung up, Jil tossed and turned in the bed. The homesickness was one element contributing to her insomnia, but so was this case. She knew who was sabotaging the aquarium, who had killed Tasha, so why did it still feel unfinished? Why did it matter what he needed the money for? Who cared?

But it felt important, like a big corner piece of the puzzle.

She got up and paced through the kitchen. After a few moments, she heard the sound of footsteps coming through the hall.

"Couldn't sleep either?" Rebecca said.

Jil turned around. "No. Too much on my mind."

"Same."

Rebecca put her arm around Jil and hugged her.

"Sorry I got you into this."

Jil pulled away and smiled. "Don't worry. It's my job."

"I didn't know you then."

"No."

"I wish I had."

Jil smiled.

Rebecca looked down. "I wish you didn't have someone waiting for you at home."

Jil took her hand back gently.

"In another lifetime," she said, "this might have worked out."

Rebecca nodded. "But not this one."

"We have our problems, but…"

"But?"

"She's my person."

Rebecca smiled. "I understand. We all need our person."

CHAPTER TWENTY-SIX

Rebecca left early the next morning, promising to come back at lunch to get Jil.

"I have more than enough paperwork to keep me busy. Some things are still bugging me, and I'll feel better once I get the file organized."

Leonard had tried to kill the whales, but had he also killed Tasha? That was the leap that she was trying to make in her mind. She was missing something—what was it?

Something about the encounter with Baz at the dock kept bothering her. Baz, son of the gendarme. Baz, the boyfriend, banging a guy at the sea aquarium. Baz, passing packages at the taxi stand. The guy was trouble, but he hadn't been around the night of Tasha's death.

At least not on camera.

When she came in from a jog on the beach, Ramone sat at the table drinking a large coffee. Emi sat on the bench next to him, having a slushie.

"Hey. Hi, kid."

He grinned at her. "I'm riding with Dad today."

"I see that."

"Boss is snowed under. She sent me to get you."

"Have they found him yet?"

"No. But she found some footage you might find interesting."

The trip to the aquarium took less than ten minutes, but Jil felt her adrenaline pumping. Ramone parked the car and they both jumped out.

"Dude!"

Ramone turned around. Max was coming up the walk, frowning.

"Hello," Jil said.

Max nodded. "I need a word with you."

"Sure," Jil said.

Ramone ducked his head and moved to pass them, his hand on Emi's shoulder. "Now remember I said you stick right with me all day. No disappearing. No going near the whales."

"Okay, Dad."

"Ramone?" Max said.

He turned around.

"Can you head down to the lagoon?"

"Why? What's up?"

"It's Koko. She's swimming slow. I can't get close enough to her to figure out what's wrong."

Ramone turned toward the dock. "Meet me there when you're done."

Jil pulled him into an alcove beside the indoor displays. "Tell me one thing."

He looked at her, frowning. "Okay. What?"

"You and Baz."

He looked down, his cheeks pink.

"How long had it been going on?"

"Not long," Max said. His voice was strained. "I didn't even know Baz was bi until one night we'd had a bit too much to drink. You know…"

"So he was cheating on Tasha with you?"

"Not really. Tasha knew he was into both."

Jil frowned. "So you never had a big fight about it?"

"And ended up shoving her into a whale tank? No."

Max moved to go around her.

"One more thing."

He looked up. "What?"

"Was Baz into drugs?"

Max shrugged. "Yeah. Maybe. I don't know. He got high sometimes, but I kinda wondered…"

"How he could afford his lifestyle?"

Max nodded.

"Are you guys seeing each other now?"

"Not really. He just wants to put this all behind him, you know? His mom's breathing down his neck. And if he were into drugs—I'm not saying he is—but with Carole around? Believe me, you want to avoid her."

Jil understood what he meant. She'd never exactly warmed to the captain.

Her brain was working out this puzzle. Somehow it fit, and somehow it just added an extra layer of questions.

Jil hurried down the hall to the office.

"Rebecca?"

She wasn't there.

She ducked out and down the other direction toward the observatory.

"Hey, what's up?" Tait asked.

"I'm looking for Rebecca."

"Oh. I saw her go down to the shark fences a few minutes ago. But the underwater ship's open so maybe she's down there."

"What's going on?"

"Beats me. They've been trying to fix a leak for the past week. Or she could be in that bathroom, or napping somewhere. Really, I have no idea."

Jil laughed. "Thanks."

Rebecca wasn't with the sharks in the outdoor holding tank that surrounded the sunken ship, but the gangplank to the ship was open, as was the hatch that led to the lower observatory. Jil walked down the gangplank and onto the deck.

"Rebecca?"

She hopped over the safety rung and down the ladder to the semi-lit lower deck. Outside, Michelangelo, the four-hundred-pound grouper, swam around, inches from the window.

Ugly looking thing.

"Rebecca?"

Above her, the hatch slammed shut, and she whipped her head up, her heart thudding painfully.

"Hello?"

No answer.

"Hello?"

She climbed back up the ladder and tried to push the hatch open, but it was shut hard.

Banging on it with her fist, she yelled for help. No one answered. She climbed back down and took out her cell phone. No bars. Of course not, in a tin can below the water. She climbed back up to the top, nearest the hatch. One bar began to flicker.

Then, down below, something started ringing. She looked around. What the hell was that noise?

An old-fashioned phone, like something in a prison visitation booth, hung on the wall. She climbed down the ladder and picked it up.

"Hello?"

"I guess you couldn't have made it easy on everyone and just drowned in the ocean."

She recognized Leonard's voice.

Where was he calling from?

"Why can't you just go away and mind your own business?" he said.

"Like let you pop off people who catch you doing naughty things? Gee, I don't know, let's call it a civic duty?"

"Yeah, well, you've failed. The plan is going ahead. So just stay down there and die this time."

A surge of anger flooded her body. "Fuck you, Leonard. Let me out of here. Do you really want to add another murder to your list of crimes?"

"I haven't murdered anyone. The whale killed that girl, not me."

"Fake news. You bashed her over the head with a hose and chucked her in the tank."

"You can never prove that."

"I can. And I will."

"Not if you're dead."

Jil held the phone with one hand and climbed back up the ladder with the other. One bar started to flicker again. Maybe not enough for a phone call, but what about a text message?

If she could keep him talking, distract him, maybe she could get help.

"If I die, you're going to have a lot of questions to answer."

"Not if nobody knows it was me. I've managed to get this far without being seen. Now all I have to do is see that you don't live to tell about it."

"That's not going to solve your money problems though, is it, genius?"

Silence.

She'd got him.

"I'd take money advice from you, possibly, if you were actually an accountant. But you're a shitty PI."

"Oh yeah? I think I've got you pretty well figured out. Here's what I think. Tell me if I'm close."

"I don't care what you know. It doesn't matter. What matters is that the glass windows on this thing are ancient, you're stuck down there, and I'm about to make sure the sea gets in."

Jil swallowed down her fear and thumbed in a message. *Trapped in the sunken ship. Help now.* She sent it to Rebecca and waited while the blue bar inched its way across the top of the screen.

"Actually, I think it matters to you a lot. Because you think you're pretty smart, but actually, you're an idiot. And when I get out of here, everyone is going to know exactly *what* a giant idiot you are. How you got yourself into gambling trouble and decided to solve that problem by committing a bunch of crimes. Embezzlement, fraud, and a drug ring come to mind."

"Everyone gambles a little. Why do you think we have so many casinos?"

"Yeah, but not everybody loses thousands, do they? Not everyone mortgages their property. So you can't pay. You really can't pay. And soon you can't even get back to the casinos to earn back your money because you have nothing to gamble with. And the guys are closing in."

"So what? So you've dug into my personal life. Congratulations. So I'm not great with my own money. Name me someone who is."

Jess, Jil thought automatically.

"Yeah, I got into a bit of debt. Sue me."

"They don't just sue you though, do they? They don't fuck around with legalities like that, right? They'd just chop off your remaining leg. Or club you. Or beat you. I mean, take your pick. That must've been scary, Leonard. Were you pissing yourself?"

"Fuck off."

"You were. I know you were. So how did you get yourself more time?"

"Who says I did?"

"I say. What did you agree to do? I have an idea, but I want to hear you say it."

The blue bar hit the right side. Gone.

"I'm not saying anything. Actually, I'm leaving. I just wanted to say good-bye."

A red circle appeared next to the message. Message not sent. Fuck.

Jil looked down. The spider web was spreading.

"This time, nobody will be able to blame me. You really have a death wish, don't you? Jumping off boats. Going down into dark holes by yourself. You'd think you'd learn."

Jil took a deep breath to calm her heart from thudding.

"You know what I think, Leonard? I think that this sea aquarium is really a perfect spot for a lot of things. Besides what it's used for, I mean."

He hesitated and she knew she was onto something. All she had to do was keep on talking.

"It's on the open water. Boats pass in and out of it all the time. Nobody thinks twice about a motorboat circling around and around here. Quick out to the buoy and back again. You know what that sounds like to me?"

"What, smart-ass?"

"A drug-smuggling opportunity."

Even as she said it, she knew she was right.

"Half a backpack of cocaine strapped to a boundary buoy. A boat passing by, taking it to another site. Bing, bang, boom."

"Great. Well, now you know. Too bad you're not going to be able to tell anyone."

She kept talking, not knowing if he was even still there. "So you decide to take some out of the accounts. Only you're not such a great embezzler and Rebecca starts to see that something's off. So you confess that you're trying something new. Trying to secure a good deal. The sea aquarium is struggling. She's happy to have a whale. You take a bit more than it actually costs. Two hundred thousand more, to be exact. And use the excess to pay off your debts.

"Only now you owe the facility two hundred thousand dollars. And you've gotta reconcile this before year end. So, how are you going to get the money, Leonard? What are you going to do?"

"I could have won it back," Leonard said.

Relief flooded her. She was still buying time. Maybe someone would see him and come running.

"Yeah, but that'll take weeks. So meanwhile, what do you do? You take up the not-so-patient guys on their offer. Smuggle in some drugs. Perfect locale. Now all you've gotta do is to kill the whale. Get your insurance. Get the drug lords off your back and get out of Dodge. So what went wrong, Leonard? How did Tasha get in your way? She found out your plan. You were trying to kill the whale and she knew."

"She should have minded her own business. I didn't kill her. It was an accident. She snuck up on me. It was Baz's fault she was even there. She walked in on us talking and she figured it out."

Baz? Baz had been there the whole time?

"So, what? You bludgeoned her?"

"She shouldn't have been there!"

"Then shoved her in the tank?"

"She would have died anyway. Her head was so banged up. It's Baz's fault. He should have made her stay in the car. None of this would have happened. They could have had their stupid date and she would still be alive."

"Head injuries bleed a lot, Leonard. She might not have been dead. You're the one who put her in the tank. She drowned."

The line went dead.

Jil slowly put her phone down in the cradle and turned around. A strange thumping noise was coming from the side of the ship.

She crept through the center observatory to the large observation window.

Whomp.

Around the pillar. Until she was face-to-face with the dense, murky underwater world outside.

A flash of gray hurtled toward the window.

Whomp.

And collided with the glass.

She stood and stared in disbelief as a shark, twice the length of her body, rammed itself against the glass. Glass that was starting to fracture.

An icy feeling spread from her head all the way to her body as she stood, rooted, watching the animal blaze out of the depths and collide with the glass. The web grew wider. Beads of water began forming along the edges.

He was one of the foremost shark trainers in the Caribbean.

Could that have included teaching a shark to ram glass?

Or a whale?

I have to get out of here.

Chapter Twenty-seven

From above deck, she heard muffled shouting. A few thumps sounded above her head, then a splash outside the porthole.

A blur thrashed by: khaki shorts, a navy top. Hairy arms and legs churning. A shoe fell to the bottom of the ocean floor, dropping from the top of the window and sinking below the ship.

"Ramone?"

His face appeared. Eyes wide. He scrambled for the surface.

Jil ran to the window and peered out, looking left and right for the shark. Why was Ramone in the water? What the hell was he doing?

Ramone surfaced then swam back down, putting his hand to the window.

A flash of gray caught Jil's eye. She gestured wildly for Ramone to surface.

"Get out! Get out!"

He swam back up.

The phone rang. Jil ignored it, her eyes glued to the porthole. But she didn't see Ramone any more. The phone kept ringing. She ran to pick it up.

"Any more of your friends come looking for you, they'll get the same greeting."

Oh God. Leonard had thrown Ramone in the water. So where was Emi?

She ran back to the porthole and looked out. No sign of the kid, but Ramone was still there. She caught sight of him swimming past the window again.

Ramone swam hard, trying to find a place to get out of the gated outdoor tank. In his panic, he missed the ladder.

The shark swam by. Jil watched, horrified, as it circled Ramone. He couldn't get out of the tank. He was going to be eaten.

"Get on the boat! Get on the boat!"

She ran around the underwater ship, trying to think. In her mind's eye, she could picture the orientation of the ship—the aft section fully sunk, the fore section rising at an angle out of the water.

She stumbled fore, a bit of an uphill climb, until she found a porthole that was just above water level. Was it big enough to squeeze through? For her maybe. Probably not Ramone. Where the hell was Emi?

A red sign caught her eye.

Fire hose. Fire extinguisher.

Where there was a fire hose, there was usually an axe.

She took off her shoe and smashed the glass case, then reached inside.

Yes. There was an axe. She grabbed it in two hands. It was heavier than she expected.

She also took the fire extinguisher.

The ship was old and brittle. The same problems that made it leak and creak would hopefully make it easier for her to get the hell out. That's what she was counting on, anyway. Her first few swings of the axe went a bit wild. Far off target. But one landed a punch right next to the porthole, and when she pulled the axe out, she saw daylight.

Using the blade to chop and, finally, the end of the axe, she busted through the porthole, dense glass shattering all around her. With her shoe, she cleared out the remaining shards that still clung to the inside of the hole.

She put her head out. "Ramone!"

No answer.

The water to her left was oozing a red stream toward her.

She shouted again. "Ramone!"

"Help! Oh God, help!" he screamed.

She ran back to the case and grabbed the fire hose, then reached through the porthole and tossed the metal end upward onto the deck, trying to lodge it tight. The first time, it came back down and almost hit her on the head. The second time, she heard it clank. When she pulled it, it stayed. She shoved the other end of the hose out the porthole and into the water, then she followed, wiggling her hips to squeeze them through the opening. Shards of glass ripped through her shorts, but she gritted her teeth and forced her way through. For a second, she held onto the inside of the porthole, terrified. The axe would be useless, but the fire extinguisher…

She yanked it through the opening and dropped to the water below.

Ramone was screaming and thrashing. And bleeding badly, by the look of things.

"Help!" she screamed, hoping somebody at the aquarium could hear her. "Help!" With the end of the fire extinguisher, she banged against the boat. The metal on metal reverberated like a gong.

"Help us!"

She listened but couldn't hear anything over Ramone's shouts.

She had to go get him. Step one was to swim under the gangplank. Step two, keep the shark away. Step three, get them both the hell out of the water.

She dove down, keeping the fire extinguisher out in front of her like a dart gun. To her left, a flash of gray made her scream, and bubbles burst out of her mouth, heading to the surface. She stopped, realizing she was wasting air. The shark passed by her and went back toward the direction of the blood. She kicked her legs fast to get under the gangplank, then surfaced to grab a quick breath. She had to get back underwater where she could see what was going on.

Ramone was panting hard, holding his arm. "Emi? Where's Emi?" he panted.

"I haven't seen him. Hope he's hiding."

The shark bumped her side and she let go a stream of foam from the extinguisher.

She surfaced again and shouted, "Come this way! Kick, Ramone. Kick. You have to follow me."

He looked at her, wide-eyed, but started side-swimming toward her.

"He took a bite of my arm," Ramone cried.

"I know. You're bleeding really bad. We have to get out of the water."

Suddenly, he shrieked. "He's got my foot!"

Jil dove under again and blasted the shark in the face with more foam. It retreated, but not far.

Jil surfaced. "We have to swim under the gangplank. There's a rope to the ship's deck.

He struggled for breath. "Okay."

Jil swam to his side, the shark circling around them. "We're going together. Big breath, and underwater. I don't know how much is left in this can."

Jil squeezed the trigger, sending off a blast of white foam as they dove under the gangplank, a flurry of kicking and bubbles, and arrived on the other side. Ramone gulped in air as soon as he came up.

"Over here," Jil shouted. He tried to follow her, but he was taking in water, sinking and choking.

Jil dropped the fire extinguisher and pulled Ramone to the side of the boat.

"Get up, fast. Fast," she shouted. He grabbed the hose with one hand and tried to pull himself up the boat, but he was bleeding and weak, and doing it one-handed was next to impossible.

"Help!" Jil screamed. "Someone help!"

A floodlight went on, somewhere above them. Boot steps boomed back and forth on the wooden deck.

"*Capitaine, ici!*"

She looked up to see the police standing on the side of the deck, flanked by Rebecca and Max.

"Get him up!" Jil yelled.

Two officers scrambled over the guardrails and hauled Ramone topside while Jil yanked herself up the fire hose.

"Holy shit," she breathed, falling onto the deck. "Holy shit."

Ramone lay beside her, blood pouring out of a massive bite on his arm.

"Papa!" Emi fell onto the deck beside Ramone and he put up his hand on his son's head.

"Thank God. Thank God," he said.

"Is he gonna die?" Emi cried.

"Snowball's chance in hell," Jil said, pressing his head into her chest.

Ramone let out an incredulous laugh that was half a groan. "I can't believe you have more I've never heard."

"He's going to be fine, Emi."

More rapid French was exchanged over Jil's head, but she didn't even try to translate as she watched an officer begin to bandage Ramone's arm.

The buzz of walkie-talkies and someone yelling for an ambulance washed over her. She lay down on the dock, her energy completely zapped.

"You're gonna need a transfusion," she said to Ramone.

He looked up at her and grinned weakly. "Did you at least catch it on camera? My viewers would love this."

Emi flopped down on his father's chest and Ramone hugged him tight.

Jil squeezed his hand. In the background, sirens wailed.

"How bad is it?"

Jil looked at the deck streaked in blood and Ramone's face, chalk-white in the fading sunlight.

"Just a flesh wound," she said.

"That's what I thought. God, this job is costing me an arm and a leg." Ramone laughed weakly, his eyes rolling back.

"Hey." Jil shook him. "Don't go to sleep."

He coughed and rasped. "Thanks for saving my life. I owe you."

"I could hardly let you die," Jil said. "I mean, what would your viewers say?"

CHAPTER TWENTY-EIGHT

Jil paced around the office at the sea aquarium, waiting for Rebecca to get off the phone. The gendarme had doubled their search efforts since they'd obviously failed to locate Leonard during their first search and he'd been on the island the whole time.

Jil stopped for a second. Baz had been involved in the drug ring with Leonard. And he'd been there the night Tasha went into the water. Which meant Baz had a lot to lose if Leonard went away.

Suddenly, everything fell into place and the penny dropped.

"I think I know where he is," she said.

Rebecca put the phone away from her ear.

"What? Where?"

"Check Baz's house."

Rebecca looked at her, stunned. "You want me to tell Carole she needs to check her son's house?"

Jil put a hand on her arm. "Trust me. That's the one place she wouldn't have looked before."

Rebecca blew out a huge breath. "If you're wrong about this…" She didn't finish that thought. Instead, she barked into the phone in French and then hung up.

"They're checking now. You can tell me on the way to the police station."

Rebecca grabbed her purse and they hurried to the jeep.

"If they find him," Rebecca said, "I want to be there when they bring him in."

They squealed out of the parking lot and onto the main street.

A few minutes later, the call came in. Rebecca answered on the car's speaker. "We've got him. He was hiding in the closet at the residence."

"Are you charging him?"

Carole's voice was clipped. "You bet your ass. You tell your friend there thanks for the tip."

Rebecca glanced at Jil. "That means she'll have to arrest her son as well," she muttered.

Jil pursed her lips. "Thanks for catching the asshole," she returned. "And hauling us out of the water. We appreciate it."

"We're even. See you soon." The line clicked off.

"How did you know?" Rebecca asked.

Jil shrugged. "Leonard had to have help on the harbor. He had to know when the harbor masters were out, where they were, what they were doing, and when the ships were coming in. He couldn't see all that from the sea aquarium. He needed a man on the inside."

"So that's why Baz has been working at the wharf. I thought it was grief over losing Tasha."

Jil sighed. "Nope. Greed. Baz had to be in on the take. I saw him do a handoff to a taxi driver the day after I got here. Leonard must have been supplying him with drugs in exchange for his information. It all makes sense now."

"But do you think he had anything to do with Tasha's murder?"

Jil shook her head. "No. I'm pretty sure that was all Leonard. Baz was there, but he wasn't the one who put her in the tank."

They pulled up to the police station in time to see Leonard, handcuffed, led into the station. They got out of the car for their front row seat.

Leonard saw Jil and his face blanched. He kept his eyes on her, even as they led him into the building, and the police officer forcibly turned his head to get him inside. Baz came next, his head down. He was visibly shaken.

"How old is that kid?" Jil asked.

"Barely eighteen," Rebecca answered. "Just wrecked his whole life."

Carole watched from the side as Baz was led into the station. She held her hat in her hand, and her face was drawn tight.

"Just a minute?" Rebecca said to Jil.

"Sure. Take your time."

She watched as Rebecca approached Carole. The way they talked, moving in each other's space so casually, so intimately. It was no question they'd once been close.

Finally, Rebecca returned and got back in the car. "Up for a drink?"

Jil buckled in. "You bet. But first a long shower, a new set of clothes…"

"And then lobster," Rebecca finished.

Jil gave her a wink. "You read my mind."

❖

That night, as Jil and Rebecca sat on the couch, watching the moon come up over the ocean, Carole called.

Rebecca switched on the video and set her tablet on the table so Jil could see.

"I was going to wait until the morning, but I thought you should know now. It's just so unbelievable."

"What is it? What did you find?" Rebecca asked.

"Well, first of all, cocaine, prescription pills, hundreds of thousands of dollars' worth of goods. But get this. We also found a dozen diagrams detailing exactly how much space is in a whale's stomach. Methods of getting whales to swallow balloons. And emails between him and another guy talking about hazmat suits and opening a whale's stomach as it's on the open water."

"What? What does that even have to—"

"Oh my God," Jil cut in. "That was his plan. That's why he wanted the whale euthanized."

Rebecca turned to her. "Why?"

Jil jumped up, almost spilling her wine. "That's how he planned to get it all off the island. I wondered how he could possibly achieve that."

"You couldn't. Not without help, and not unless you had a serious blind eye from the harbor masters," Carole said. "Which, unfortunately, is possible. But it would be very expensive."

"Right," Jil said. "The amount of debt he was in, he couldn't afford to pay anyone on the take, or risk anyone knowing about his plan. That left him with an awful lot of drugs to get off the island unnoticed."

"Yes," Carole put in triumphantly.

Rebecca looked at her like she'd landed from another planet.

"Think about it—what do you do with a whale carcass?" Jil said.

"Well, normally we'd send it for scientific study—"

"If you didn't know what killed it. Or if you did?"

"Take it out to the ocean. Let the marine life take care of it."

"Which would make it the perfect vessel for hundreds of pounds of smuggled drugs, wouldn't it?"

"You're not serious." Rebecca's jaw dropped. "Get the whale to swallow the balloons. Dump the whale's body in the ocean. Somebody comes to rendezvous, collect it. C'mon, really?"

"Desperate times call for desperate measures." She instantly thought of Ramone.

"How much did you say he owed in debts?"

"A cool two million dollars."

Rebecca sat back. "Two million dollars. How do you even get that far in debt?"

"I don't know, but with the guys who are going to be after him, he'd better hope he's going to land in jail for a long time."

"For murder? I'd say he's going away for life."

"Carole, how is Baz?" Rebecca asked.

Carole glared. "He's dead. That's how he is."

Jil and Rebecca exchanged a look.

"Sorry for what you're going through," Jil said.

Carole took a deep breath. "Thank you. And I'm sorry for being a...well, you know."

"As you said, we're even."

"I'll see you soon," Rebecca said, and they disconnected.

Jil smiled and stood up to clear the drinks from the table. "And now that this is over, I'm going to plan my flight home."

Rebecca stood too, bringing the plates to the counter. "I can't thank you enough for your help."

"What are you going to do with the sea aquarium?"

"Well, actually...I've decided to let the protestors help."

"Really?"

"Crazy, right? They'll raise money to buy the orcas and we'll send them to an ocean sanctuary. But the dolphins and the sharks are staying. We're going to continue with the therapy program, minus the picketers. I think it'll be okay. Ramone said he's got some ideas for marketing on social media."

Jil laughed out loud. "You've seen him?"

"This morning."

"Wait till he tells you all the details. You're going to love it."

"Come on. I'll drive you back to your hotel. You can enjoy one last night of peace and quiet on the island, minus any death threats."

"That will be great."

As Jil and Rebecca hopped out of the Jeep outside Jil's hotel, a motorcycle roared to a stop beside them, and the driver took off her helmet.

Jil's gaze went from the tight leather coat to the short brown hair. It took her a second to recognize the captain of the gendarme, minus her uniform.

"Ready?"

Rebecca smiled and took the extra helmet that Carole offered her.

"See you around, Jil. Your check is already at your headquarters in Rockford."

Rebecca hopped on the back of the motorbike and wrapped her arms around Carole's waist. With a crank of the throttle, Carole kicked it into high gear, leaving Jil staring and chuckling to herself.

Chapter Twenty-nine

Jil checked her watch for the thirtieth time and decided to take one last walk down to the harbor before she went back to her hotel and got ready to catch the next flight out of here.

Ten days on a tropical island had deepened her tan and all the beach walking had strengthened her legs, but she missed home. It was time to get there. She chucked all her clothes in a suitcase and hailed a cab.

But she had one more stop to make first.

Ramone was sitting up in bed when she entered the room.

"You're alive!"

"I am. And I hear you caught the canary. Congratulations." His right arm was bandaged in multiple layers of gauze and slung to his shoulder, but his color had improved a lot since the last time she'd seen him.

Jil rolled her eyes. "How many pints of blood did you need?"

"I don't know. I was afraid to ask. A lot. They have me on some good pain meds. I can hardly feel my toes. But the bite will make for some good viewing when these bandages come off." He grinned.

"I hear your YouTube channel is about to become official. Way to go!"

"It's already taking off like a rocket ship. I posted this morning about the shark attack, and the story's already got thousands of views."

Jil punched his good arm. "Thanks for coming to save me."

He rolled his eyes. "Yeah, well, thanks for saving my ass in the end. Shark versus fire extinguisher. Who knew?"

Jil laughed. "Hey, listen, I didn't have a lot at my disposal!"

"You're dressed up. You're not heading out?"

"Yeah, just on my way to the airport now. My girlfriend's husband just died. I've got to get home."

Ramone nodded. "Too bad. Sorry to hear. But thanks for everything. Come back soon for an actual vacation, would you? We'll put you up and everything."

"I don't know. The way this vacation turned out, I think maybe I'll be shooting for Europe next!"

Ramone lowered his voice. "I hear there aren't many good sharks there."

She kissed his head and said good-bye. "Let me know when you go viral. I want to pop a bottle of champagne."

He waved as she got to the door. "I'll miss you around. But absence makes the heart grow fonder."

Chapter Thirty

S till not here," Father Makarios said, his frown deepening. Jess paced around the anteroom. Her feet clacked loudly on the old wooden floors, and she didn't miss the effect on her former students. They looked at each other, eyebrows raised.

"There's a huge accident on the highway, Miss. Maybe she got stuck."

With a distracted nod, Jess paced to the door, peeked out, and shut it again.

"We have a substitute canter," Father Makarios said. "She can do everything except the offertory hymn, which she doesn't know."

"That's the most important one," Jess whispered back. "Everything else I guessed at. That one, he chose." Tears kept clouding her eyes, and she fought to stay standing. Moving forward.

The mourners were beginning to grow restless in the pews. The funeral was supposed to start at ten. It was now ten fifteen.

The back door opened, and Jess turned around. When she saw Jil standing there, her knees went weak, and she had to lean against the back of a chair.

"How did you make it back?" she asked. In a black dress and heels, no less.

"Red-eye through Florida," Jil replied.

They looked at each other for a long moment. Jil wouldn't approach unless Jess made the first move. An implicit agreement, and one that had never hurt her more than at this very moment.

She held out her hand and Jil grasped it tightly, once, before letting go.

"Miss Kinness?" said one of the students.

Jil turned around and smiled. For the day, she'd don the persona of the teacher she'd impersonated for those four months she was undercover at St. Marguerite's.

"In the flesh," she replied.

"What are you doing here? I thought you left."

"I did. But Mr. Blake was a friend of my family."

She looked at Jess, and Jess could barely suppress a sob.

Father Makarios strode back through the doors. "I've set up the substitute canter at the podium. I'm afraid that's the best I can do."

The students heard their cue in that statement and grabbed their offerings before lining up to proceed.

Jess hung back and Jil took her arm. "What's the problem?" she whispered.

"The canter's stuck in traffic or something," Jess replied. "I'll be playing a cello solo of 'His Eye is On the Sparrow.'"

Jil frowned. "How long till the hymn?"

With a quick glance at the clock, Jess replied, "About twenty minutes. Maybe twenty-five."

Jil looked toward the door. "I'll see if I can locate her."

"Would you?"

"'Course."

Jess paced and wrung her hands until she had no choice but to walk down the aisle behind Mitch's coffin. She was the widow. She had a role to play. Myra was already waiting in the front pew and Jess slipped in next to her as the pallbearers lifted Mitch up onto the platform.

For the opening prayers and hymns, she continually checked behind her to see if the canter had arrived, but no.

And then, as suddenly as the service had started, the priest was performing a blessing and it was time for the offertory.

Jess walked over to the podium, her heart hammering so loudly she was surprised it didn't thump over the microphone.

She warmed up a bar, trying to stop the trembling of one hand.

This was it. The canter wasn't going to make it. Tears clouded her vision, and she blinked fast, trying to see the music. She couldn't fall apart right now. She couldn't.

She lifted her bow and played the first chord.

Beside her, heels clacked on the podium. She glanced sideways and saw Jil standing beside her.

"Is she here?" she whispered.

Jil shook her head.

Jess took up her bow. Damn. What a failure. Her eyes filled with tears again. This was the one request he'd made and she couldn't even give it to him. With a shaking hand, she played the introductory bars, then heard the microphone beside her click off its stand.

Jil began to sing.

"Why should I feel discouraged? Why should the shadows come?"

For a second, Jess almost stopped playing. In the acoustics of the church, Jil's voice was a rich, melodic hum that balanced and flew on the wings of Jess's cello. A gift she'd never before heard Jil share. She almost missed the next note, but forced her attention back onto the page and kept playing.

The mourners stared as Jess and Jil worked their way through the song, Jil following her lead—a musical partnership that stunned Jess even as she played through to the end.

She set down her bow, and Jil stepped down from the podium beside her, finding her seat several rows back.

"Let us pray," the priest intoned.

❖

Jil handed Jess an empty glass before curling up next to her on the couch. The fire was on full blast in the hearth, winter having decided to overstay its welcome as usual in Ontario.

Zeus grunted and made his way up onto the middle of the couch, wiggling and huffing until he'd found his perfect spot.

"Careful of the champagne," Jess said, holding the bottle high out of reach.

They had the laptop open on the coffee table, watching Ramone's YouTube channel views tick upward every minute. At the current rate, it would go over a million in the next few minutes.

Jil passed her the bowl of popcorn.

"Which video is this?"

"The one where he reenacts what happens underwater when you fire an extinguisher, then shows his shark bite."

Jess pointed at the screen. "It's happening. Look. Get ready!"

Jil picked up the bottle of champagne and unscrewed the tie.

"One more view. Okay, now!"

Jil popped the cork and it hit the ceiling.

Zeus barked as bubbles fizzed all down Jil's arm and onto the couch.

"Shit. Pass me that—"

But Jess was already mopping up the mess with a tea towel.

Jil poured them each a glass and they toasted Ramone.

"So Padraig says you've been busy."

"Indeed. I was working on two cases at once. Quite a revelation."

Jil kissed her hand. "Because you're brilliant and we couldn't do without you, obviously."

"Well, Padraig needed me to help him catch a thief, which I did, thank you very much. Mostly using what you taught me from our resident thief at St. Mag's."

"Ugh. Asshole who stole your ring?"

"Exactly. So I have to thank you partially for that one. Also, I think Padraig was missing you. He said at least three times that he wished you were over in Ireland with him."

"Did he? It sounds like he's really retiring."

Jess took a sip of her wine. "I know."

Sadness clouded Jil's face. "What am I going to do without him?"

"You could buy him out," Jess suggested quietly. "You have the money."

Jil shook her head. "I know. But what would I do without *him*? Who would back me up?"

Jess held out her glass. "I've been thinking...I'd like to. I think I'd be good at it."

Jil sat back. "Really? You would work with me? And live with me?"

"Yeah. I think we'd be a good team, don't you?"

Jil pulled Jess closer to her and snaked her arm up the front of Jess's shirt. In a second, she'd taken it off her, and Jess reached over and pulled Jil's tank over her head. They lay together, kissing in the light of the fireplace, the soft blanket entwined around them as Jil's fingers entwined Jess's hair.

On Jess's tongue, Jil tasted the Burgundy. "My house sold today."

"Did it?"

"So now this is actually our loft."

Jil pulled back and smiled. "We're going to be a hell of a team."

"Nothing was the same without you," Jess whispered.

"Same."

"I'm sorry I didn't..."

Jil propped herself up on her elbow, tracing a line down Jess's sternum, between her breasts and over to circle one nipple.

"What?"

"Let you in. Let you help. I just…I had to finish what I started. And I disappointed him so much in our marriage that I couldn't…"

"Bring your new lover to his bedside? I understand."

"You do?"

"I do. I will admit that I was hurt. And that it took me a while to get it. But I do now. I'm sorry there was a time I wasn't in your life. That you were so confused and heartbroken. But I'm here for you now and that's not going to change."

Jess kissed her again and ran her hands up Jil's back.

"Welcome home."

Zeus hopped down from the couch with a grumble and flopped down on his dog bed.

Jil chuckled. "Sorry, buddy."

But Jess's mouth was busy making her forget having ever been away from home, and she closed her eyes as her head started swimming.

"I love you, Jillienne Kidd."

"I love you too. Partner in crime."

About the Author

Stevie Mikayne is the author of *UnCatholic Conduct* and *Illicit Artifacts*, both finalists for the Lambda Literary Award. She holds an MA in creative writing and is currently pursuing her PhD from Lancaster University (UK). Toting their laptops and photo blogging equipment, Stevie and her small family are on a 437-day adventure that involves seeing their native Canada, traveling on a shoestring budget, homeschooling their five-year-old daughter, and spending time in their second home, Curacao, where a lot of the research for this book was done. You can follow them at BungalowToBohemia.com.

Books Available from Bold Strokes Books

A Wish Upon a Star by Jeannie Levig. Erica Cooper has learned to depend on only herself, but when her new neighbor, Leslie Raymond, befriends Erica's special needs daughter, the walls protecting her heart threaten to crumble. (978-1-163555-274-4)

Answering the Call by Ali Vali. Detective Sept Savoie returns to the streets of New Orleans, as do the dead bodies from ritualistic killings, and she does everything in her power to bring them to justice while trying to keep her partner, Keegan Blanchard, safe. (978-1-163555-050-4)

Breaking Down Her Walls by Erin Zak. Could a love worth staying for be the key to breaking down Julia Finch's walls? (978-1-63555-369-7)

Exit Plans for Teenage Freaks by 'Nathan Burgoine. Cole always has a plan—especially for escaping his small-town reputation as "that kid who was kidnapped when he was four"—but when he teleports to a museum, it's time to face facts: it's possible he's a total freak after all. (978-1-163555-098-6)

Friends Without Benefits by Dena Blake. When Dex Putman gets the woman she thought she always wanted, she soon wonders if it's really love after all. (978-1-163555-349-9)

Invalid Evidence by Stevie Mikayne. Private Investigator Jil Kidd is called away to investigate a possible killer whale, just when her partner Jess needs her most. (978-1-163555-307-9)

Pursuit of Happiness by Carsen Taite. When attorney Stevie Palmer's client reveals a scandal that could derail Senator Meredith Mitchell's presidential bid, their chance at love may be collateral damage. (978-1-163555-044-3)

Seascape by Karis Walsh. Marine biologist Tess Hansen returns to Washington's isolated northern coast where she struggles to adjust to small-town living while courting an endowment for her orca research center from Brittany James. (978-1-163555-079-5)

Second in Command by VK Powell. Jazz Perry's life is disrupted and her career jeopardized when she becomes personally involved with the case of an abandoned child and the child's competent but strict social worker, Emory Blake. (978-1-163555-185-3)

Taking Chances by Erin McKenzie. When Valerie Cruz and Paige Wellington clash over what's in the best interest of the children in Valerie's care, the children may be the ones who teach them it's worth taking chances for love. (978-1-163555-209-6)

All of Me by Emily Smith. When chief surgical resident Galen Burgess meets her new intern, Rowan Duncan, she may finally discover that doing what you've always done will only give you what you've always had. (978-1-163555-321-5)

As the Crow Flies by Karen F. Williams. Romance seems to be blooming all around, but problems arise when a restless ghost emerges from the ether to roam the dark corners of this haunting tale. (978-1-163555-285-0)

Both Ways by Ileandra Young. SPEAR agent Danika Karson races to protect the city from a supernatural threat and must rely on the woman she's trained to despise: Rayne, an achingly beautiful vampire. (978-1-163555-298-0)

Calendar Girl by Georgia Beers. Forced to work together, Addison Fairchild and Kate Cooper discover that opposites really do attract. (978-1-163555-333-8)

Lovebirds by Lisa Moreau. Two women from different worlds collide in a small California mountain town, each with a mission that doesn't include falling in love. (978-1-163555-213-3)

Media Darling by Fiona Riley. Can Hollywood bad girl Emerson and reluctant celebrity gossip reporter Hayley work together to make each other's dreams come true? Or will Emerson's secrets ruin not one career, but two? (978-1-163555-278-2)

Stroke of Fate by Renee Roman. Can Sean Moore live up to her reputation and save Jade Rivers from the stalker determined to end Jade's career and, ultimately, her life? (978-1-163555-162-4)

The Rise of the Resistance by Jackie D. The soul of America has been lost for almost a century. A few people may be the difference between a phoenix rising to save the masses or permanent destruction. (978-1-163555-259-1)

The Sex Therapist Next Door by Meghan O'Brien. At the intersection of sex and intimacy, anything is possible. Even love. (978-1-163555-296-6)

Unexpected Lightning by Cass Sellars. Lightning strikes once more when Sydney and Parker fight a dangerous stranger who threatens the peace they both desperately want. (978-1-163555-276-8)

Unforgettable by Elle Spencer. When one night changes a lifetime… Two romance novellas from best-selling author Elle Spencer. (978-1-63555-429-8)

Against All Odds by Kris Bryant, Maggie Cummings, M. Ullrich. Peyton and Tory escaped death once, but will they survive when Bradley's determined to make his kill rate one hundred percent? (978-1-163555-193-8)

Autumn's Light by Aurora Rey. Casual hookups aren't supposed to include romantic dinners and meeting the family. Can Mat Pero see beyond the heartbreak that led her to keep her worlds so separate, and will Graham Connor be waiting if she does? (978-1-163555-272-0)

Breaking the Rules by Larkin Rose. When Virginia and Carmen are thrown together by an embarrassing mistake they find out their stubborn determination isn't so heroic after all. (978-1-163555-261-4)

Broad Awakening by Mickey Brent. In the sequel to *Underwater Vibes*, Hélène and Sylvie find ruts in their road to eternal bliss. (978-1-163555-270-6)

Broken Vows by MJ Williamz. Sister Mary Margaret must reconcile her divided heart or risk losing a love that just might be heaven sent. (978-1-163555-022-1)

Flesh and Gold by Ann Aptaker. Havana, 1952, where art thief and smuggler Cantor Gold dodges gangland bullets and mobsters' schemes while she searches Havana' s steamy Red Light district for her kidnapped love. (978-1-163555-153-2)

Isle of Broken Years by Jane Fletcher. Spanish noblewoman Catalina de Valasco is in peril, even before the pirates holding her for ransom sail into seas destined to become known as the Bermuda Triangle. (978-1-163555-175-4)

Love Like This by Melissa Brayden. Hadley Cooper and Spencer Adair set out to take the fashion world by storm. If only they knew their hearts were about to be taken. (978-1-163555-018-4)

Secrets On the Clock by Nicole Disney. Jenna and Danielle love their jobs helping endangered children, but that might not be enough to stop them from breaking the rules by falling in love. (978-1-163555-292-8)

Unexpected Partners by Michelle Larkin. Dr. Chloe Maddox tries desperately to deny her attraction for Detective Dana Blake as they flee from a serial killer who's hunting them both. (978-1-163555-203-4)

A Fighting Chance by T. L. Hayes. Will Lou be able to come to terms with her past to give love a fighting chance? (978-1-163555-257-7)

Chosen by Brey Willows. When the choice is adapt or die, can love save us all? (978-1-163555-110-5)

Death Checks In by David S. Pederson. Despite Heath's promises to Alan to not get involved, Heath can't resist investigating a shopkeeper's murder in Chicago, which dashes their plans for a romantic weekend getaway. (978-1-163555-329-1)

Gnarled Hollow by Charlotte Greene. After they are invited to study a secluded nineteenth-century estate, a former English professor and a group of historians discover that they will have to fight against the unknown if they have any hope of staying alive. (978-1-163555-235-5)

Jacob's Grace by C.P. Rowlands. Captain Tag Becket wants to keep her head down and her past behind her, but her feelings for AJ's second-in-command, Grace Fields, makes keeping secrets next to impossible. (978-1-163555-187-7)

On the Fly by PJ Trebelhorn. Hockey player Courtney Abbott is content with her solitary life until visiting concert violinist Lana Caruso makes her second-guess everything she always thought she wanted. (978-1-163555-255-3)

Passionate Rivals by Radclyffe. Professional rivalry and long-simmering passions create a combustible combination when Emmett McCabe and Sydney Stevens are forced to work together, especially when past attractions won't stay buried. (978-1-163555-231-7)

Proxima Five by Missouri Vaun. When geologist Leah Warren crash-lands on a preindustrial planet and is claimed by its tyrant, Tiago, will clan warrior Keegan's love for Leah give her the strength to defeat him? (978-1-163555-122-8)

Racing Hearts by Dena Blake. When you cross a hot-tempered race car mechanic with a reckless cop, the result can only be spontaneous combustion. (978-1-163555-251-5)

Shadowboxer by Jessica L. Webb. Jordan McAddie is prepared to keep her street kids safe from a dangerous underground protest group, but she isn't prepared for her first love to walk back into her life. (978-1-163555-267-6)

The Tattered Lands by Barbara Ann Wright. As Vandra and Lilani strive to make peace, they slowly fall in love. With mistrust and murder surrounding them, only their faith in each other can keep their plan to save the world from falling apart. (978-1-163555-108-2)

Captive by Donna K. Ford. To escape a human trafficking ring, Greyson Cooper and Olivia Danner become players in a game of deceit and violence. Will their love stand a chance? (978-1-63555-215-7)

Crossing the Line by CF Frizzell. The Mob discovers a nemesis within its ranks, and in the ultimate retaliation, draws Stick McLaughlin from anonymity by threatening everything she holds dear. (978-1-63555-161-7)

Love's Verdict by Carsen Taite. Attorneys Landon Holt and Carly Pachett want the exact same thing: the only open partnership spot at their prestigious criminal defense firm. But will they compromise their careers for love? (978-1-63555-042-9)

Precipice of Doubt by Mardi Alexander & Laurie Eichler. Can Cole Jameson resist her attraction to her boss, veterinarian Jodi Bowman, or will she risk a workplace romance and her heart? (978-1-63555-128-0)

Savage Horizons by CJ Birch. Captain Jordan Kellow's feelings for Lt. Ali Ash have her past and future colliding, setting in motion a series of events that strands her crew in an unknown galaxy thousands of light years from home. (978-1-63555-250-8)

Secrets of the Last Castle by A. Rose Mathieu. When Elizabeth Campbell represents a young man accused of murdering an elderly woman, her investigation leads to an abandoned plantation that reveals many dark Southern secrets. (978-1-63555-240-9)

Take Your Time by VK Powell. A neurotic parrot brings police officer Grace Booker and temporary veterinarian Dr. Dani Wingate together in the tiny town of Pine Cone, but their unexpected attraction keeps the sparks flying. (978-1-63555-130-3)

The Last Seduction by Ronica Black. When you allow true love to elude you once and you desperately regret it, are you brave enough to grab it when it comes around again? (978-1-63555-211-9)

The Shape of You by Georgia Beers. Rebecca McCall doesn't play it safe, but when sexy Spencer Thompson joins her workout class, their non-stop sparring forces her to face her ultimate challenge—a chance at love. (978-1-63555-217-1)

www.ingramcontent.com/pod-product-compliance
Lightning Source LLC
Chambersburg PA
CBHW022015010726
47494CB00003B/1046